Shunshō Tamenaga

The Loyal Ronins

An Historical Romance

Shunshō Tamenaga

The Loyal Ronins
An Historical Romance

ISBN/EAN: 9783337348557

Printed in Europe, USA, Canada, Australia, Japan

Cover: Foto ©Andreas Hilbeck / pixelio.de

More available books at **www.hansebooks.com**

THE LOYAL RONINS

AN HISTORICAL ROMANCE, TRANSLATED FROM THE JAPANESE

OF

TAMENAGA SHUNSUI

BY

SHIUICHIRO SAITO AND EDWARD GREEY

ILLUSTRATED BY

KEI-SAI YEI-SEN, OF YEDO

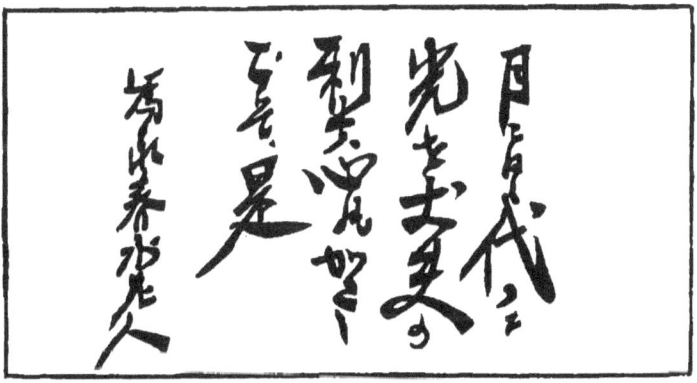

" This is the Legacy of the Loyal Samurai. The friction of Time, which obliterates
most things, adds lustre to their fame."

TAMENAGA SHUNSUI
(OLD MAN)

NEW YORK
G. P. PUTNAM'S SONS
182 FIFTH AVENUE
1880

The illustrated cover of this book was designed and drawn by Mr. Edward Greey.

INTRODUCTION.

The brilliant display made by Japan at the International Exhibition at Philadelphia gave an impetus to the interest already excited among Western nations concerning Japanese art, and from that time the subject has commanded the wonder and admiration of the world. Indeed, at no distant period, the names of Hokusai and of the Kano Brothers are destined, like those of Raphael and Hogarth, to become household words in every American and European family.

The literature of a people and their works of art are signs by which the student is enabled to learn the degree of civilization and refinement attained by a nation, and it cannot be denied that the Japanese, who have achieved so much in art, possess a literature of no mean order.

Foremost in the ranks of her celebrated writers are Bakin and Tamenaga, and the Western world, which has already acknowledged the genius of Hokusai and of the Kano Brothers, will not fail to appreciate the wit and pathos to be found in the writings of the authors whose names I have quoted.

For many reasons, which I need not here mention, the works of our writers have been sealed to American and English readers. It is true, in "Mitford's Tales of Old Japan," something has been related of the social condition of the people; but as an example of Japanese literature, the book possesses little value. Within the last ten years the pages of the "Japan Mail" have contained many articles of great interest; however, few persons are aware of the existence of such a periodical.

Three years ago I determined to translate a standard Japanese novel, and thus supply a want I knew was greatly felt by those interested in my country.

After some thought I decided to take the "I-ro-ha Bunko" of Tamenaga; first, because he is one of the most popular of our writers; secondly, on account of the romance containing a wonderful description of Japanese life under the feudal system, and of an institution, which, for more than seven hundred years, has exerted a most powerful influence over the nation.

Notwithstanding many misrepresentations and expressions of disgust heaped upon Roninism, I feel sure those who have written upon the subject have only seen "one side of the picture." While I am the last person to defend lawless acts, I cannot avoid feeling a certain admiration for the much-despised institution, believing that it contained the germ of patriotism.

The author and book having been decided upon, I, in the summer of 1879, began my task; but finding myself unequal to the work, sought and obtained the assistance of an estimable lady residing in Boston. Although I had her hearty and sympathetic coöperation, I failed to make satisfactory progress and we abandoned the attempt.

In October, my attention was called to the Japanese stories of Mr. Edward Greey, of Manchester, Mass., which greatly delighted me, they giving most graphic, amusing, and instructive descriptions of the manners and customs of my countrymen, and showing the author's thorough familiarity with our literature. I wrote to him at once, and our acquaintance, so interestingly begun, soon ripened into friendship. I discovered Mr. Greey had not only lived many years in the East, and knew Japan from Yezo to Kiusiu, but that he is also an accomplished Japanese artist. During the following January, I mentioned to him my attempt with "I-ro-ha Bunko," when he recognized the work and agreed to join me in its translation. The result is before the reader.

To those who have assisted Mr. Greey and myself, I tender my most hearty thanks, especially to Mr. Gilbert Attwood, of Jamaica Plain, Mass., who has for many years been a sincere friend to Japan and the Japanese, and without whose kind and generous surrender of his copy of "I-ro-ha Bunko," we would not have been able to complete this translation. To Mrs. Edward Greey, who so kindly copied the MSS. for the printers, I return my best thanks; also to Mr. Makoto Fukui, of New York, and Mr. A. Van Name, Librarian of Yale College, for the loan of copies of Tamenaga's works; and to Mr. John A. Lowell, of Boston, who has done so much to bring Japanese art before the public, and who so freely gave us the use of his library of Japanese books.

I feel especially happy in being able to offer this trifling tribute of my gratitude to the American people, with whom I have lived for the last five years, and in one of whose institutions of learning I have received the education of which, I hope, with the help and guidance of the spirits of my ancestors, I shall make good use in the service of my sovereign and country. Wherever I have been I have received a most kind welcome, and the memory of the generous hospitality extended to me will always be retained in my heart.

By the time this work reaches you I shall be crossing the broad Pacific on my way home, yet I trust the day is not far distant when I shall again be among you to study more thoroughly your noble institutions, which are founded upon the principles of freedom I so greatly love and admire. Till then I say *Sayonara* (farewell).

SHIUICHIRO SAITO.

Manchester-by-the-Sea, Mass.,
July 19, 1880.

NOTES.

"The Loyal Ronins" is one of seven stories written by Tamenaga Shunsui (For-the-sake-of-perpetual Spring-water), and published under the title of "I-ro-ha Bunko" ("The A B C Writing-desk"). The edition used by Mr. Saito and myself bears the imprint of Nakamura-ya Kozo (Middle-village-store Happy-store-house) of Yedo, and was issued in parts, at irregular periods, between the seventh year of Tempo (Heaven-secure) and the first year of Kayei (Fortunate-perpetual)—A.D. 1836–1848. It is in eighteen volumes, containing over a hundred and eighty illustrations by Kei-sai Yei-sen (Valley-cottage Superior-spring).

Tamenaga founded the modern school of Nihonese fiction, and was the Charles Dickens of Japan.

The author's arrangement of the romance, while perfectly intelligible to a Japanese, would, if literally followed, have utterly bewildered our readers—Tamenaga taking for granted that his patrons were thoroughly acquainted with the story of the forty-seven ronins. We were therefore compelled not only to rearrange the sequence of the chapters, but to supply the links in the story omitted by the author.

These were obtained by referring to "Ako Shijiu hichi-shi Den" (The Biography of the Forty-seven *Samurai* of Ako), "Sei-chu gi-shi mei-mei ga-den" (The Pictorial Biography of the Truly Loyal *Samurai*), and other works.

We have endeavored to reproduce Tamenaga's romance without making use of foot-notes or those stumbling-blocks to readers, Japanese names for persons and places. These are, in nearly all instances, translated literally. In the cases of individuals either the surname, the given name, or the military title is used. Our reason for retaining Japanese words, such as *samurai, ronin, sambo, saké,* etc., was the impossibility of translating them concisely.

The original illustrations are in two pieces, an arrangement peculiar to Japanese works, and one that, to the Western eye, totally destroys the effect of the pictures. Before reproducing the engravings I was compelled to unite them and retouch the lines of junction.

Some of the half-cuts were engraved independently of the others, and no amount of ingenuity would make them join correctly.

Many very interesting pictures had to be rejected on account of their not having any connection with the letter-press.

Those who are acquainted with the Japanese language will fully understand the difficulties we had to overcome in preparing this work for the press, and none better than ourselves know its imperfections. We have not attempted to translate the quaint sentences into elegant English, but have done our utmost to retain the unique, naïve style of the author, believing it were "best to leave well alone."

If this specimen of Nihonese literature pleases our readers, we are prepared to give them other works by Tamenaga, and the romances of Bakin, the Sir Walter Scott of the Japanese literary world.

EDWARD GREEY.

Manchester-by-the-Sea, Mass.
July 19, 1880

エ
ド
ワ
ル
ド
・
グ
リ
ー

AUTHOR'S PREFACE.

During the long winter evenings of my childhood, when the lamp burned dimly in the paper
lantern and but partly revealed the pictures on the
screens, I often sat by the fire-bowl and listened
with awed face to my honored mother, who, to com-
pensate me for the gloom of the apartment, would
relate stories of the Forty-seven Ronins, and thus
illuminate my soul with the light of loyalty. It was
from her honored lips I received the histories em-
bodied in this work ; therefore, if the book pleases,
I beg the reader not to think of the old man of
Yedo whose brush traces these characters, but to
pay grateful respect to the spirit of my honored
parent, whose eloquent descriptions I have so imperfectly reproduced, and whose body is now resting
beneath the tall grass.

CONTENTS.

xi

xii   *Contents.*

THE LOYAL RONINS.

CHAPTER I.

UNSHEATHING THE SWORD.

In the month of November, A.D. 1698, during
the reign of the Shogun Iyetsuna, the president of
the Council of Elders in Yedo, was officially informed
that three commissioners were on their way from
the Imperial Court at Kioto, and was directed to appoint two officials to receive them ; in consequence
of which he nominated Lord Morning-field of Ako,
and Lord Tortoise-well, *daimio* (great lords) of equal
rank, who were instructed to place themselves under the
orders of Kira, Master of Ceremonies to the Shogun.
This man, not being a *daimio*, lacked the true
principles of nobility : was greedy, corrupt, and insolent in the discharge of his duties, treating the
customary presents brought by the lords with scorn
and addressing them in terms of undisguised contempt. At first they bore his behavior with quiet
dignity, however, when it became insufferable, they
determined to resent it and even went the length of
resolving to kill him.

Sir Reedy-plain, the chief councillor of Lord
Tortoise-well, learning of his Lord's annoyance secretly visited Kira, and bribed him with offerings
which he diplomatically represented came from his
master, and thus averted evil from their house.

Sir Big-rock, chief councillor of Lord Morning-
field, was less fortunate. When he heard his chief
had been appointed one of the officials to receive
the commissioners he felt troubled, knowing, as he
did, the reputation of the upstart Kira, besides
which, being in charge of the castle of Ako, in the
province of Harima, distant nearly three hundred
miles from Yedo, he could not leave his post and
personally propitiate the Master of Ceremonies.

After pondering over the matter, he summoned a
samurai (knight or military gentleman) of the clan,
named New-well, to whom he said

" I wish you at once to start for Yedo, on most
important business.   Are you ready to go ? "

" Yes, sir, yes," was the response.   " I am always
at your service, at any moment, day and night? "

" Very good," said Sir Big-Rock, adding, in a
lower tone, " I have here a letter and some money
that I desire swiftly conveyed to our lord's councillors, Sir Arrow-stand and Sir Wisteria-lake.   The
communication instructs them to wait privately on
Kira, and hand him the gold, two hundred *rio* (dol-
lars), as though it came from our chief.   I have written urging them, on no account to neglect this duty,

as by so doing they might expose our lord to serious
annoyance ; " then, giving him a smaller package
containing fifteen *rio*, continued, " This sum will be
sufficient to defray your travelling expenses. I am
sure you will not fail speedily to discharge this important commission."

Sir New-well bowed respectfully and after receiving the letter and money, said :

" I am honored by your selecting me for this responsible duty ; please accept my thanks. I will do
my utmost in return for your great favor."

Before the sun had set the faithful *samurai* was on
his way, and he traveled day and night until he arrived at his destination.

Unfortunately for Lord Morning-field his councillors, Sir Arrow-stand and Sir Wisteria-lake, were
men of little intelligence, parsimonious in their ideas
and stupid in the execution of their duties. Upon receiving Sir Big-rock's letter they hesitated to carry
out his commands, deeming the money would be as
good as thrown into the bay. Therefore, when their
chief next presented himself to Kira he was treated
with neglect and covert disdain, while Lord Tortoise-
well was welcomed with obsequious flattery and carefully initiated in his duties.

On the morning the commissioners were expected
from Kioto the two lords proceeded to the castle of
Oshiro for the purpose of receiving their final instructions. Kira, after complimenting Lord Tor-

toise-well, turned to the latter's companion and said :

" Here, my Lord Morning-field, the string of my sock has become loosened. Tie it for me."

Although the noble's patience was almost exhausted, he complied with the insolent command, deeming it an imperative duty to obey the representative of the Shogun, at the same time resolving, later on, to seek Kira and demand satisfaction at his hands.

After awhile the Master of Ceremonies excused Lord Tortoise-well, who was permitted to retire to the reception hall. Then, addressing the other noble more contemptously than before, he said :

" How exceedingly clumsy you are to-day. One would think you were a countryman, ignorant of the manners of Yedo."

At this provocation Lord Morning-field rose, and, clutching the hilt of his sword, cried:

" Defend yourself, Sir Kira, I will no longer submit to your unjust treatment."

Instead of bravely drawing his weapon and facing his challenger, Kira trembled and endeavored to escape, whereupon the noble dealt him a blow that, had it not been for the cap worn by the official, would have cleft his head in twain. Kira, finding himself wounded, uttered loud cries, and, pressing his hand to his forehead, rushed away, hotly pursued by Lord Morning-field who, as his victim fled, once more attacked him, but missing his aim, buried his weapon in

"Defend yourself, Sir Kira! I will no longer submit to your unjust treatment!"

Chap. i, p. 4.

a pillar behind which the fugitive had retreated. The incensed noble was following him up when an officer arrived on the scene, and advancing behind the *daimio*, threw his arms around his waist, thus giving Kira ample time to escape.

An hour afterward Lord Morning-field was commanded to retire to his residence and consider himself under arrest.

CHAPTER II.

HOW A DAIMIO MET HIS DEATH.

"The *man-rio* is developed and beautified by the snows of winter. Injustice to the lord reveals and intensifies the devotion of the *samurai*."

Thus wrote the Lord of Ako one lovely morning in December, two weeks after his encounter with Kira. The noble, costumed in his official garb, was kneeling before a writing table in his study engaged in verse-making, his manner betraying no anxiety concerning the impending decision of the Council of Elders. Upon the desk were some volumes of poetry, an ink-stone bearing his crest, falcon's feathers crossed and enclosed in a circle, some brushes resting on a lacquered holder and a small kettle of inlaid metal containing water with which to moisten his ink.

He grasped the slender bamboo-stemmed writing-brush firmly and formed the characters with a swift motion. Then, when he had completed the poem, turned his head and glanced into the veranda, where

The *man-sie* (Ten-thousand-golden-berry plant).
Chap. II, p. 6.

stood a porcelain flower-pot containing the object of his inspiration, a *man-rio* plant, upon the bright green leaves of which was piled the snow of the previous night, contrasting charmingly with the clusters of ruddy berries hanging beneath. As he gazed upon this the rising sun sent its rays across the scene and made the crystals sparkle like a cluster of stars.

While the master of the house was thus calmly employed, his retainers were moving silently about their duties. No song came from the kitchen, no voice was heard speaking above a whisper. The main gate was closed, a temporary fence of green bamboo had been built before it—a sign the lord was a prisoner—and a friend of the family, surety for the chief, gave orders and decided who should enter or quit the mansion. A great sorrow was upon the household and all, save its head, trembled with apprehension.

In the midst of his reverie, a screen behind him was moved noiselessly aside and Lady Fair-face, his wife, entered the apartment ; her features too plainly betraying the disturbed state of her soul. Advancing toward him she sank upon the floor and bowing until her forehead touched the mat, said in an agitated voice :

"I trust my lord is in the enjoyment of good health."

The noble regarded her tenderly and replied

" I am well, Fair-face ; why are you so sad? "

The lady conquered her grief and said :

" My lord, when you are in danger, how can I appear happy ? "

Although her words moved him he did not betray any emotion, but inviting her to approach nearer, pointed to the poem.

Lady Fair-face read it slowly, and glancing at him, remarked :

" Ah, my lord, you are prepared for the worst! Kira is all powerful with the Shogun, and his friends will do their utmost to crush the house of Ako."

" Have no fear, Fair-face! My greatest anxiety is on your account. I know what is passing in your mind. Your actions have betrayed you."

" My actions, my lord ? "

" Yes," indicating the *man-rio.* " You cannot deceive me. Last evening, when you tended that plant, you used one of your hair-pins to remove a dead berry and left the trinket on the rim of the vessel, also your paper handkerchiefs near it—they are there this morning."

" How forgetful of me," she murmured, gazing sadly at him. " I can deceive all the world but you."

Uttering these words she leaned forward, and placing her hands on his knees, rested her face upon them. The noble glanced sorrowfully at her and laying his hand on her shoulder, said :

" Fair-face, the bird driven from its nest always finds some shelter from the storm. Whatever may occur, I desire you will place implicit confidence in my chief-councillor and regard his words as though they were mine. When I succeeded to the rank and estates of

my honorable father, I imagined myself wiser than
Big-rock, however, I quickly discovered my error and
learned to value him at his true worth. He is a man
of a hundred thousand, brave, honorable, fertile in resource, patient under difficulties and a thorough statesman."

" Statesman!" she cried. " Ah, then why has he
not averted this danger 'from us? Kira was most
polite to Lord Tortoise-well."

Lord Morning-field did not reproach her for this
wifely outburst, merely replying

" I am certain Big-rock has done his duty. If harm
overtakes our house it will not be through any fault or
neglect of his. He is a mirror of loyalty. I pray you
not to forget my estimation of him."

The lady bowed her head and clung to her husband,
knowing full well that she was soon to part from him
for ever. Lord Morning-field endeavored to comfort
her and when she became somewhat composed, led
her toward the entrance to her apartments, saying

" Fair-face, I will send for you later on. I understand, you have passed a sleepless night—lie down
and endeavor to seek refreshment in slumber."

She tottered into the passage-way and sinking upon
the floor saluted him, sobbing as though her heart
would break. Lady Pine-island, her chief attendant,
advanced quickly and drawing the screens between
the rooms, shut the pitiful sight from her lord's view.

The noble slowly returned to his desk, and kneeling

before it, remained in profound thought until the hour
of the Dragon (8 A.M.), when he was disturbed by
the entrance of Sir Common, who, prostrating himself
near the doorway, announced the arrival of the Commissioners from the Shogun.

Lord Morning-field arose and quitted the study,
passing Sir Common who was still respectfully upon
his hands and knees and who presently followed him.
Upon reaching the main entrance the noble received
and gravely saluted his visitors, whom he conducted to
the reception hall where they seated themselves in the
place of honor ; he kneeling on the mats, lower down,
the apartment, facing them.

Neither of the officials spoke nor returned his salute,
they being there as the representatives of the Sho-
gun.   After a moments pause, the elder drew a
folded document from his bosom, and extending it
toward the noble, said :

" My Lord Morning-field, we are ordered by the
Shogun to announce the decision of the Council of
Elders in the matter of your unsheathing your sword
within the precincts of the castle of O-shiro.   We request you will at once read and carry out this decree."

The noble gravely received the paper and having
reverently lifted it to his forehead, calmly perused its
contents, then addressing the commissioners, said :

" This commands me to commit self-despatch and
announces the confiscation of my estates and extinction
of my family name, to all of which I most respectfully
submit."

The chief commissioner listened with unmoved countenance and replied :

" In that case we are ready to act as your witnesses."
Lord Morning-field, who had not anticipated any other judgment, summoned Sir Common and bade him remove some screens concealing a recess in the hall, when the visitors beheld the preparations necessary for the solemn ceremony. He advanced to the place and removing his outer garments revealed the *shiromuku* (white suit used during mourning and sacrificial ceremonies) after which he seated himself on the thick mats and signaled Sir Common to summon Sir Pure. When the latter had entered, bowed and taken his place behind his chief, Lord Morning-field, addressing the commissioners, remarked :

" With your permission I will give my final instructions to my councillors."

No objection being offered to this he bade Sir Common approach close to him, then pointing to a white pine-wood box resting on a *sambo* (stand) of like material, whispered in his ear ; presently drawing a letter from his bosom and handing it to the *samurai*, who listened with the deepest attention and, after his lord had ceased to speak, saluted him reverently and retired to his left hand.

The scene was most impressive. In the centre of the group knelt the noble, calm and resolute, before him were seated the commissioners, cold and stern, and behind him crouched the faithful *samurai*, ready to render the last services to their chief.

Outside the mansion all was still, there being a light covering of snow upon the ground. Inside reigned a dead silence for, though the retainers set their teeth and clenched their fingers in agony, no sound escaped their lips.

Lord Morning-field gazed through the open screens upon the beautiful view beyond and, mutely bidding it farewell, calmly reached for the dirk placed near his right hand.

*   *   *   *   *   *   *

That afternoon a mournful procession wended its way toward the cemetery of the Spring-Hill Temple in the southern suburb of Yedo. In the midst of the cortege was borne a *norimono* (enclosed litter) containing the dead body of the Lord of Ako, which was conveyed to its final resting place amid the tears, lamentations and prayers of thousands of people.

CHAPTER III.

THE MOTHER OF SIR STRAIGHT-GROVE.

" The hungry, persistent fly quickly discovers a dead body.
The great man's misfortune fattens the news-seller."

This was said, many years ago, by a learned man of
Kioto who had thoroughly studied human nature, and
these words equally apply to our own time.
Early on the morning of the day after the tragedy,
the city of Yedo swarmed with men shouting themselves hoarse in their endeavors to dispose of news-
sheets containing full particulars of the death of the
Lord of Ako. In one hand they carried their paper
lanterns and in the other the broad-sides which had
been printed during the night. After awhile their
cries aroused the inhabitants, who quitting their beds
hastened into the streets and, as they made their pur-
chases, eagerly inquired if the latter contained an account of the self-despatch of Sir Kira.
" What are you asking ? " laughingly exclaimed one
of the venders, a merry-looking boy who had folded

his pocket-towel and secured it on the top of his head, as a protection against the dew, and whose muddy clogs indicated he had traveled from the suburbs. " Do not expect too much! My honorable masters, you will find your fifteen cash worth of horrors in this sheet. One seldom discovers two nuts in a single shell."

" When will Sir Kira die ? " demanded an old man, who wore horn-spectacles and was nervously fumbling in his bag for coins. " I am anxious to know, as I have relations in the clan of Ako."

The news-seller comically rolled his eyes and stuck out his tongue, then replied :

" Don't worry yourself—Sir Kira will die a natural death."

This announcement amazed the listeners who were fully aware of the law, which required that equal pun-ishment should be meted out to all parties engaged in a quarrel.

At the hour of the Horse (noon), the people learned Kira was to escape with the loss of his office and a few days nominal imprisonment, on hearing which they became very indignant and secretly condemned the partiality of the Shogun.

Among the minor instructions, contained in the de-cree sentencing the Lord of Ako to self-despatch, was one directing that the three residences of the *daimio* in Yedo were to be given up to commissioners accredited by the Shogun, who would take possession of them within two days of the noble's death. This news

" My honorable masters, you will find your fifteen-cash worth of
horrors in this sheet."

Chap. iii, p. 14.

spread consternation in the hearts of the clansmen residing in the city; they, in the absence of Sir Big-rock, being at a loss how to act in such a sudden emergency. By the mandate a thousand families were rendered homeless, and as they entirely depended upon the annual allowances received from their lord, their situations were pitiful in the extreme. Some, who lacked the true spirit of loyalty, disposed of their effects and took service under new masters ; however, the greater number, after attending to the immediate wants of their families, packed their armor and set out for the castle of Ako.

Everything was in confusion and loud were the lamentations of the women who, unlike their husbands, did not hesitate openly to denounce the severity of the sentence, which not only ended the life of their chief, but broke up their homes and deprived them of subsistence.

One of the unfortunates was a *samurai* named Straight-grove, whose aged parent had been the foster-mother of the dead lord. On the day of his death she visited his residence in order to bid farewell to his body, and upon seeing the sad sight became frantic with grief. Lady Fair-face, fearing the old woman would do herself some injury, commanded Sir Straight-grove to conduct her home, which he did with many expressions of tenderness and affection. After awhile his words appeared to comfort her and she recovered her usual calmness of manner, whereupon her delighted son softly retired to the kitchen and poured out a cup of *saké* (rice wine), which, having placed on the family altar, he drained to soothe his agitated nerves.

When the members of his household returned from the funeral, he assembled them and announced that they were to depart on the morrow for his brother's residence in the province of Izu, at the same time stating he would proceed to join Sir Big-rock at the castle of Ako.

As that was to be their last night in the old home, he directed his wife to prepare a little feast, and about the hour of the Rooster (6 P.M.), they gathered in the dining-room and partook of various delicacies which the careful house-wife had made with her own hands. His mother appeared heartily to enjoy the viands and when the children went to bed, cheerfully remarked to her son :

" Our time here grows short so I will seek my room and do some writing."

All present bowed respectfully, and Sir Straight-grove said :

" Honorable mother, I trust you will sleep well."

When, later on, he retired for the night he saw the lamp was still burning in her apartment and knew she had not sought her bed.

The next morning the family rose earlier than usual and began to pack their effects, even the little ones assisting, but no sound came from the chamber of the grandmother. Sir Straight-grove, imagining she was

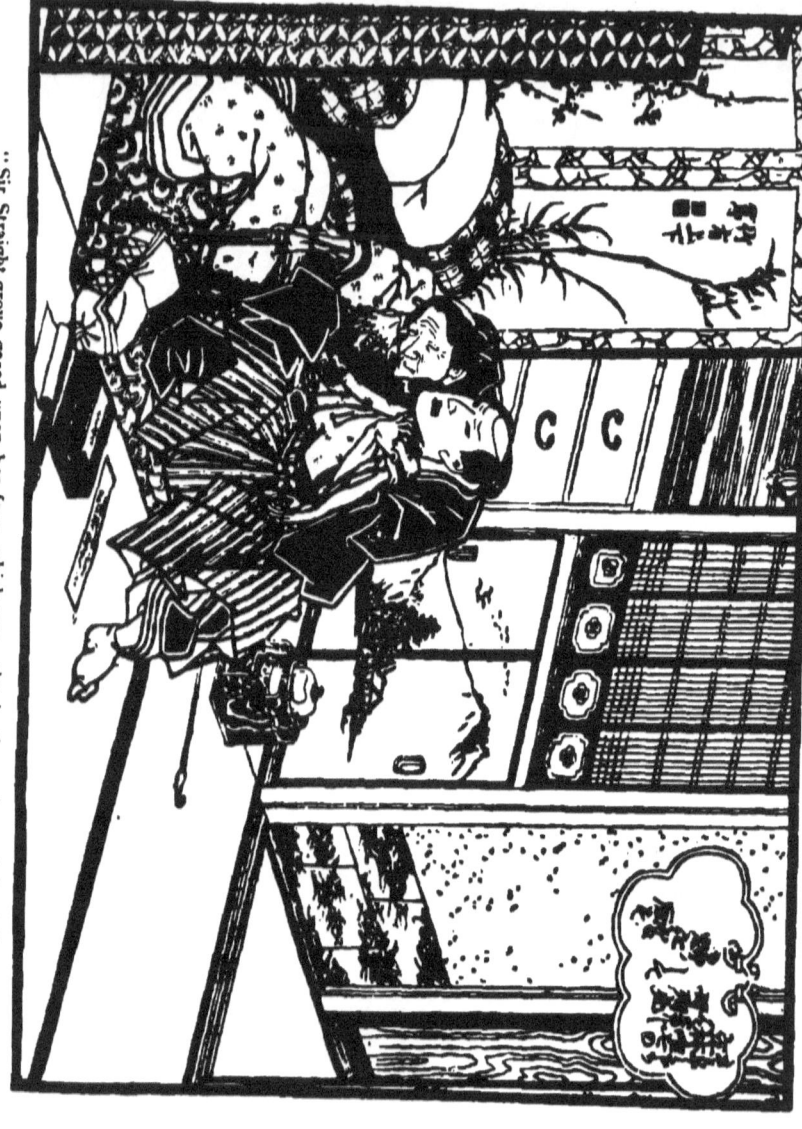

Chap. iii, p. 17.

" Sir Straight-grove gazd upon her face, which was calm in the majesty of death."

tired through sitting up late, refrained from disturbing her; however, as the hours passed and she did not make her appearance, he grew uneasy and approaching the door of the room, knocked gently, saying

" Honorable mother, I pray you will make haste to arise. It is very late and the bearers are waiting outside to convey your baggage to Izu. Excuse my thus rudely summoning you.

He paused and listened for a reply. Receiving none he became thoroughly alarmed and drawing back the sliding door entered the apartment, then moving toward the bed, pushed aside the screen, saying:

" Honorable mother—!"

To his horror he saw her face was unnaturally white and the bed-clothes were crimson with blood.

" What !" he exclaimed, as he tremblingly surveyed the shocking sight. " Was my mother crazy that she should do this? Alas for me !"

Advancing and weeping bitterly, he knelt, raised her in his arms and gazed upon the placid face, calm in the majesty of death. As he held her left hand in his and supported her with his right, he beheld the weapon with which she had ended her life ; its appearance plainly denoting the will and courage that had sustained her last moments—a courage worthy of the mother of a brave *samurai*.

His lamentations quickly attracted the members of his family who crowded into the room, and falling upon their knees, saluted the dead.

By the side of the mat, which had proved an altar for her loyal sacrifice, was a writing-case, and near it a folded paper inscribed ;

"LAST WORDS."

When the body had been removed from the room, Sir Straight-grove noticed the letter and proceeded to read it, stopping every now and then to wipe the tears from his blinded eyes.

This was the communication, written in a firm hand by the heroic matron :

" I leave you a few words. To-day a dreadful calamity overtook our lord and I have almost lost myself. When he entered the world my hands received him. My tongue taught his to say *uba* (nurse—literally milk-mother). ˑ It was I who watched his infant steps and my heart that swelled with pride when he first walked the length of a mat. I saw him bloom into childhood and develop into a glorious youth. I was present, behind the screens, when he first received the clansmen in public audience, when his consummate tact, dignity and manhood, brought tears to my aged eyes. He was my foster-son, my chief, my lord. Therefore, to-day, when I saw his murdered body, I determined he should not, unattended, travel the Lonely Road. I am about to end my life in order that my spirit may accompany his on its journey. When our lord hears the sound of my clogs behind him he will be comforted, knowing in death as in life, his old nurse is in attendance upon him.

" My son, my heart dwells upon you, although I can but feebly express my thoughts. As you read this, grasp the hilt of your sword and swear swift vengeance upon the enemy of our master—vengeance which will cause you to follow me so quickly that I shall hear behind me the echoing of your clogs and ere long welcome you to the land of shadows.

" In my closet, wrapped in a purple cloth, are three volumes of a novel I borrowed from Mrs. Moat Jr. You will return them with my thanks. I also desire you will give two of my robes and one of my girdles to my maid, Miss Angel.

" Take good care of your health until the day arrives for you to avenge our master, when you will not consider yourself.

To my dear son,

From your mother."

Sir Straight-grove dropped the document, and grinding his teeth with rage, presently exclaimed :

" Who is the cause of all this ?   Is it not solely due to the insult Kira offered my honored master ?   I call the gods to witness he shall not escape punishment."

When the day of retribution arrived Sir Straight-grove was the first to cross swords with the retainers of Sir Kira.

CHAPTER IV.

" *To-o ke moya*
Ikura to-o kumo nani kamaya senu
Yeube no furi de mizu ga mashi
Masu nomi dekiru kio no kawa bito."
" May the distance between the banks of the river
be great. What is troubling you ? The water is high
through the storm of last night, and our fares being
high in proportion, we can afford to indulge in big
cups of *saké.*"

Such was the song chanted by a number of lightly-
clad coolies, whose occupation consisted in carrying
passengers and vehicles across the Kagosa river,
which formed the eastern boundary of Harima. They
were a turbulent, lawless party, the terror of solitary
travelers from whom, notwithstanding the instructions
of the village elders, they generally contrived to ex-
tort more than the legal amount of fare. Some of
them were squatting on the banks smoking and gabm-
ling, others stretched upon their backs dozing or

20

watching the rays of the setting sun that gilded the swift waters of the stream, while the rest stood waist-deep in the flood and amused themselves by splashing their comrades.

As they were thus employed one of the party, shading his eyes with his hands, espied two travelers signaling them from the opposite bank, on seeing which he exclaimed :

" A great beauty is making signs to me from the other side of the river. I will hasten over and attend to her."

" What is that? What is that? " cried the others, springing to their feet. " A beauty—who is she ? "

Instead of replying, the fellow rushed into the water and began to breast the stream, laughing and shouting :

" I am coming, great lady, I am coming."

The other coolies followed him like a flock of ducks anxious to secure a choice morsel.

The object of their attention was a charming girl of eighteen with a complexion like a *momo* (peach-flower), whose costume and manner denoted her to be the daughter of a *samurai*, and who was accompanied by a young man-servant, armed with one sword. The attendant remained a few paces behind his mistress and anxiously watched the coolies. Night was coming on, the banks of the river were almost deserted, the place had a bad reputation and the *yakago* (cylindrical net of split bamboo filled with stones, used as an embankment) cast a deep shadow on the spot where they stood and hid them from the view of approaching travelers.

On came the men and presently the foremost, emerging from the water, staggered up the slippery incline, shouting ;

" Come, young lady, mount on my shoulders, the stream is deep and no one can carry you as easily as myself."

The frightened maiden shrank from him and would have fled, when he rudely seized her and endeavored to raise her from the ground, As he did so another coolie quitted the water, exclaiming :

" Look here, man. I am already engaged by that lady! You shall not rub your unshaven chin against her pearly face."

" Here, boys," cried the third, a tall, muscular wretch. " It is useless for you to make love to her. Cannot you see she prefers me ? Among the gallants of the Kagosa river who is better looking than I ? " and tearing her from the embrace of his companion, he continued " Don't flutter so, my little crow, I will carry you safely over the rough water."

On hearing this outrageous speech, her servant, no longer able to restrain his indignation, threw down her baggage and rushing into their midst, rescued his mistress, then drawing his sword, exclaimed :

" Dogs, what do you intend to do ? My lady is not alone, I am here to defend her. Dare again to lay a finger upon her and you will experience the consequences."

The coolies stared as though amazed at his audacity and seizing their cudgels fell upon the brave lad, whom they beat and kicked cruelly, after which their leader seized the young lady and made off with her, followed by his triumphant companions. Ere they had gone many paces a *ronin-samurai* was seen approaching along the road, noticing which they halted and clustered around their victim. The face of the newcomer was concealed by a straw hat that effectually masked his features, and at the same time permitted him to see ; like a person who peeps behind the grating of a prison,

This stranger was Sir Unconquerable, a man whose name fitted him like his *tabi* (socks) and who, some years before, had belonged to the clan of Ako. One day having purchased a sword, he had thoughtlessly tried its temper upon an impertinent peddler whose friends brought the matter to the notice of his chief. Although the latter admired the bravery of his follower and greatly valued his services, he could not condone his offence, so giving Sir Unconquerable a sum of money, he dismissed him and the knight became a *ronin* (wave-man, one who, though still a *samurai*, owes allegiance to no master).

Such was Sir Unconquerable who, on seeing the young lady in the hands of her captors, advanced, seized them one after the other by their hands, twisted them like broken bamboos and hurled them to the ground, having done which he turned to the affrighted maiden and said :

" The atrocious conduct of these scoundrels must have sorely troubled you."

The young lady was too much agitated to reply, however, her servant who, spite of his wounds, had risen to his knees, said ;

" Honorable Sir, you have indeed arrived at an opportune moment."

Sir Unconquerable placed his hand upon the hilt of his sword, and advancing upon the prostrate coolies, exclaimed :

" Much to be hated dogs, prepare for death."

The fellows made off like birds alarmed by a hunter or ants whose nest is disturbed by a husbandman.

The young lady and her servant, overjoyed at their escape, knelt before their deliverer, folded their palms and expressed their gratitude, the lady saying :

" Sir stranger, accept my profound thanks."

" And mine," murmured the servant. " Though my spirit sprung like an arrow, I was alone and could do but little to defend the daughter of my master. Through your bravery we have escaped a great danger. The gratitude of your humble servant knows no bounds We expect to meet my master in the next village when we will, without fail, present ourselves at your residence and thank you for your kindness. Be pleased to let me know your honorable name ? "

Sir Unconquerable listened grimly and replied :

" I do not require such thanks for so trifling a mat-ter. Do not trouble yourself further about this, but conduct your mistress back to the nearest inn, the sun will soon be set."

" You are very kind," said the young lady. " Still I would much like to know to whom I am indebted for my deliverance."

While she and her servant were urging him to di-vulge his name, they heard loud voices proceeding from the other side of the river and presently beheld a host of travel-stained coolies, carrying a light litter and running with all their might. As this party plunged into the stream a second one was seen in the distance.

Sir Unconquerable watched the approach of the pro-cession, and as the first litter was borne up the bank, glanced at its occupant and said :

" Pardon me, but is not the honorable *samurai* who travels post-haste, Sir Common of the clan of Ako ? "

The person addressed ordered his bearers to halt a moment, then said :

" Strangely met, Sir Unconquerable."

" Sir Common," said the former, approaching the litter, " your manner of traveling alarms me. Has any harm befallen my lord ? "

Sir Common pointed to a little frame fixed in the front of the litter, on which was secured the *sambo* and white pine box, referred to in a former chapter, and said :

" Your fears are well founded. We have, in five days, traveled nearly three hundred miles to convey this," bowing respectfully, " to Sir Big-rock and announce to him the great calamity that has overtaken our lord. You must excuse my relating the particulars ; you will learn them from Sir Pure who is following me."

Ere he had uttered the last word, the bearers once more lifted the litter and starting at a run, vanished in the direction of Ako.

The *ronin*, too impatient to wait for the arrival of the second litter upon the bank, waded into the river, approached the vehicle and shouted

" Sir Pure, Sir Pure, it is I, Unconquerable! I pray you tell me what misfortune has occurred to our lord? "

Sir Pure waited until his bearers had carried him alongside the speaker, when, placing his mouth close to Sir Unconquerable's ear, he whispered the sad news, adding :

" We have made up our minds what to do. If you still remember the gracious favors of your late lord, you will not hesitate to join us."

Sir Unconquerable, who, as he spoke, waded by the side of the litter, answered :

" Sir Pure, it is not necessary you ·should remind me of such a thing. Although my spear is somewhat rusty and my armor dilapidated, I can make good use of them."

Sir Pure hastily saluted him and they ascended the bank, on reaching the summit of which the bearers

broke into a run and rapidly followed the other litter ; leaving Sir Unconquerable with the young lady and her attendant.

For some moments he remained as though lost in thought, the sad fate of his lord, profoundly affecting his loyal soul. He felt that, beginning with Sir Big-rock, all the *samurai* of the clan should die defending the castle against the army of forfeiture, and, as he turned to conduct the strangers to a place of safety, did not notice the dim outlines of the trees and rocks, but only beheld the *sambo* and white pine box carried in the litter of Sir Common.

When they arrived at the office of the road-com-missioners, in the little village near the ferry, he made a formal complaint against the coolies, then, requesting the officers to take care of the travelers and see them to an inn, returned to his humble lodging, where he took his armor from its rest and busied himself in mending and polishing it.

The next morning he disposed of his few effects and started on foot for Ako.

CHAPTER V.

" Better have a dishonest servant than a stingy
one," was the golden maxim of the ancients, by
which they meant, he who is too careful with his master's money, often becomes the means of ruining him.
Meanness is not economy. The unpardonable failure of
Sir Arrow-stand and Sir Wisteria-lake to pay over
the gold sent by Sir Big-rock as a bribe for Kira, was
treason against their lord and indirectly the cause of
his death.

After the chief councillor had despatched Sir New-
well, he felt somewhat easy in his mind and looked
with little apprehension for the return of his
messenger. Therefore, imagine, if you can, his grief
and indignation when he heard the awful news
brought by Sir Common and Sir Pure, who reached
Ako upon the night of their meeting Sir Unconquerable on the bank of the Kagosa river.

When Sir Common handed the letter, entrusted to
him by his dead chief, to Sir Big-rock, the latter

28

raised it reverently to his forehead, then with trembling fingers essayed to break the seal. As he did so he beheld the *sambo* and pine box from which Sir Pure had removed the white covering; whereupon the chief councillor, unable to restrain his grief, bowed his head to the mat and wept, his emotion being shared by the messengers.

After awhile he conquered his sorrow, and addressing Sir Common, said :

" I trust the spirit of our lord will forgive my exhibition of weakness. These are the only tears I will allow myself."

Thus speaking he opened the letter and slowly perused its contents, and having thanked the exhausted messengers for their loyal devotion in hastening to carry out the instructions of their chief and given directions that their wants should be attended to, dressed himself in his robes of ceremony, and taking the *sambo* and its sacred burden in his hands, proceeded to the castle where he deposited his charge on the *tokonoma* (raised recess corresponding to our mantlepiece), and that accomplished, sent out couriers to summon the clansmen to an extraordinary council.

While awaiting their arrival he knelt, motionless as a statue, with his eyes fixed upon the white pine box, thinking how he should best carry out the wishes of his lord. Presently his hand sought the bosom of his robe and he drew from it the letter, which he again read ; the communication being as follows :

"THOU KNOWEST."

This was signed with the military name of the late noble.

In a short time the clansmen began to assemble, each, as he arrived, silently taking his place on the matted floor according to his rank and respectfully saluting the chief councillor, their blanched faces and grave looks plainly denoting the anxiety that possessed their souls. The hours passed slowly as they knelt, mute and mournful, with their right hands grasping the hilts of their long swords, which they held vertically and used to support their bent bodies.

The first gray streaks of dawn were illuminating the horizon when an aged soldier ascended the castle-tower, and approaching the big bell sorrowfully drew back the suspended beam used as a clapper and swung it against the metal ; repeating his action seven times and thus proclaiming the hour of the Tiger (4 A.M.) After he had completed his task he leaned over the parapet, and placing his withered hand to his wrinkled ear listened, presently muttering to himself

"The last of the clansmen has come in. I hear the warden closing the great gate. Now the council will begin."

His surmise was correct. At that moment Sir Big-rock raised his head and announced the reason for so suddenly assembling the members of the clan.

The news fell upon the *samurai* like a thunderbolt upon an egg. A dead silence reigned in the apartment, and the dumbfounded clansmen glanced at one another as though utterly unable to comprehend the full meaning of the communication. After awhile one of the juniors uttered a cry of indignation. Then a loud clamor arose all over the hall and, notwithstanding their respect for the chief councillor, everybody spoke at once.

"Now is the moment to remember the golden words of the ancients," excitedly exclaimed a young *samurai* "When the master is insulted it is for the servant to die. Our lord is no more, therefore let us follow him, dying gallantly defending his castle, the ramparts of which shall be our pillow. Sir Chief-councillor, this is our determination, frankly spoken. How and when it is to be accomplished, we leave to your decision."

Sir Big-rock understanding their excitement permitted them freely to express themselves. Then once more calling the meeting to order, said ;

"Fellow clansmen, your exhibition of loyalty, while admirable in its intent, savors too much of haste. You desire to die like true *samurai*. Where is your enemy to be found? It will be easy enough to throw away your lives but the height of folly to sacrifice yourselves without obtaining some return. Our duty is to petition the authorities to appoint Lord Great-learning, the honored brother of our late master, chief of our clan and thus restore the house of Ako. As yet we only partially know the decision of the council of elders.

I expect, as our lord was directed to commit self-despatch, Sir Kira, unless he has already died of his
wound, will have received a similar sentence. This
matter was not known on the afternoon of our lord's
death when Sir Common and Sir Pure left Yedo. I
propose we despatch two competent persons to the
capital for the double object of presenting the petition
and ascertaining the fate of Sir Kira. How say you,
fellow clansmen?"

The assembly almost unanimously signified its assent, then Sir Moat, Sr., addressing the president,
said :

" Sir Chief-councillor, there is one matter to which
I desire to call your attention. I understand when
you heard of the danger likely to overtake our late
lord, you gave certain instructions to his councillors in
Yedo, which, if carried out, would have averted this
calamity. They, without doubt, failed in their duty
and their treasonable neglect should be punished with
death at our hands."

" Yes, with death at our hands," echoed the clansmen.

Sir Moat, Sr., paused until the sound of their voices
had died away, when he continued

" Sir Chief-councillor, I trust you will assent to this."

Sir Big-rock bowed gravely, after which he turned
to Sir Shell and Sir Pigeon-field, and said

" I shall have to trouble you with the mission to
Yedo. You will travel post-haste and return in the

same manner.   Fellow clansmen," once more addressing the assembly, " from to-day until further orders,
you will remain in the castle, every one at his post,
and the clan will be ready under arms.   We will now
close the council."

The members saluted and retired, and before night
the castle was in a state of complete defense, every
one anxiously waiting for information from Yedo.

Two days afterward Sir New-well arrived post-haste
from the capital, bringing news of the sentence passed
upon Sir Kira.

This announcement caused the whole clan to grind
their teeth and say :

" There is now no hope for us, however we will not
be cowards and bring upon ourselves the ridicule and
contempt of the world.   We will fight and die, and our
bodies, hanging over the ramparts, will show that we
deserve the name of loyal *samurai*.   Although the clan
of Ako may no longer exist, people will say ' the
master who observes his duties, shall have servants
who do the same.'   This is the only return we can
render for the well-remembered favors of our dead
lord."

Filled with these lofty sentiments, the whole clan
swarmed to the castle, each carrying his armor, swords
and spear, eager to be the first to enter the portal and
report himself for duty.

CHAPTER VI.

THE CLANSMEN PREPARE TO DEFEND THE CASTLE.

"The beautiful lotus springs from the mud.
Loyalty knows no distinction of rank."

This ancient maxim admirably describes the feeling that animated the clan of Ako. It is true, on hearing of their lord's misfortune, some of the *samurai* had sought safety in the service of other masters; however, these were exceptions, the majority of the clansmen, including the foot soldiers, forgetting all else but their duty, loyally rallying round the standard hoisted by the chief-councillor.

Sir Big-rock, ever wise and watchful, placed certain officers at the castle gate with instructions to take down the names of all who presented themselves and assign them duty according to their rank and merit.

Among those who approached the portal, were three *ronin-samurai* whose appearance plainly betrayed their spirit and determination. These men had some time before lost the good will of the lord of Ako. Instead of obtaining service elsewhere they had wandered about

"The Castle of Ako, Province of Harima, on the shore of the
inland sea."

Chap. vi, p. 34.

the country, waiting for the day when he would forgive them and restore them to their former positions.
Upon hearing of his fate they had vowed to die in his
cause, and although their armor was rusty and their
clothes ragged, hastened to present themselves before
the registering officers.

" Wait a moment, if you please," remarked the latter. " While admiring your spirit I cannot permit
you to enter the castle, the orders of the chief councillor excluding all but clansmen from enrollment."

Sir Cliff-field, speaking for the others, replied

" Honorable Sir, you are quite right, yet, though
only *ronin*, we are determined to die for our lord ;
therefore, be good enough to report our presence to
Sir Big-rock. If you do not grant us this favor we will
end our lives where we stand."

The official did as he was requested. In a few moments a messenger came out, and after thanking the
three *ronin*, in the name of Sir Big-rock, presented
them with money and clothing, then, taking down their
addresses, said :

" You may, at some future day, hear from the chief-
councillor. At present he is unable to avail himself of
your services."

Upon hearing this decision Sir Cliff-field, unable to
restrain his tears, replied in a husky voice :

" The kindness of Sir Big-rock is well known to us.
Taking pity upon our wave-like fortune he, even in
the hour of his trial, forgets not to remember our needs.

Under these circumstances we dare not refuse his bounty or disobey his order to withdraw. We most sincerely trust, when his plans are decided upon, he will communicate with us."

The others added their entreaties to his, and after the messenger had promised to inform the chief-councillor of the same, they departed, commenting upon the goodness of Sir Big-rock.

During the succeeding days the registering officers were kept busily employed by the arrival of the loyal clansmen from Yedo, in addition to whom came merchants from the city and farmers from the provincial villages, who, catching the loyal spirit of the clansmen, were anxious to offer their services.

In the midst of the bustle there appeared a very poorly clad. man, carrying on his back a set of dilapidated, purple armor and bearing in his hand a formidable spear. He advanced without any demonstration and attempted to enter the portal, noticing which the registering officer contemptuously motioned him to retire, remarking with a sneer :

" We have no occasion for your services."

His words were caught up by the bystanders who began to mock the new-comer ; one of them saying :

" Look at the fellow's clothes! I wonder at his impudence in desiring to be registered ; it would be good for him to take a glance in a mirror."

" O, don't you understand ! " said another. " He fears to die of hunger, so wishes to enter the castle

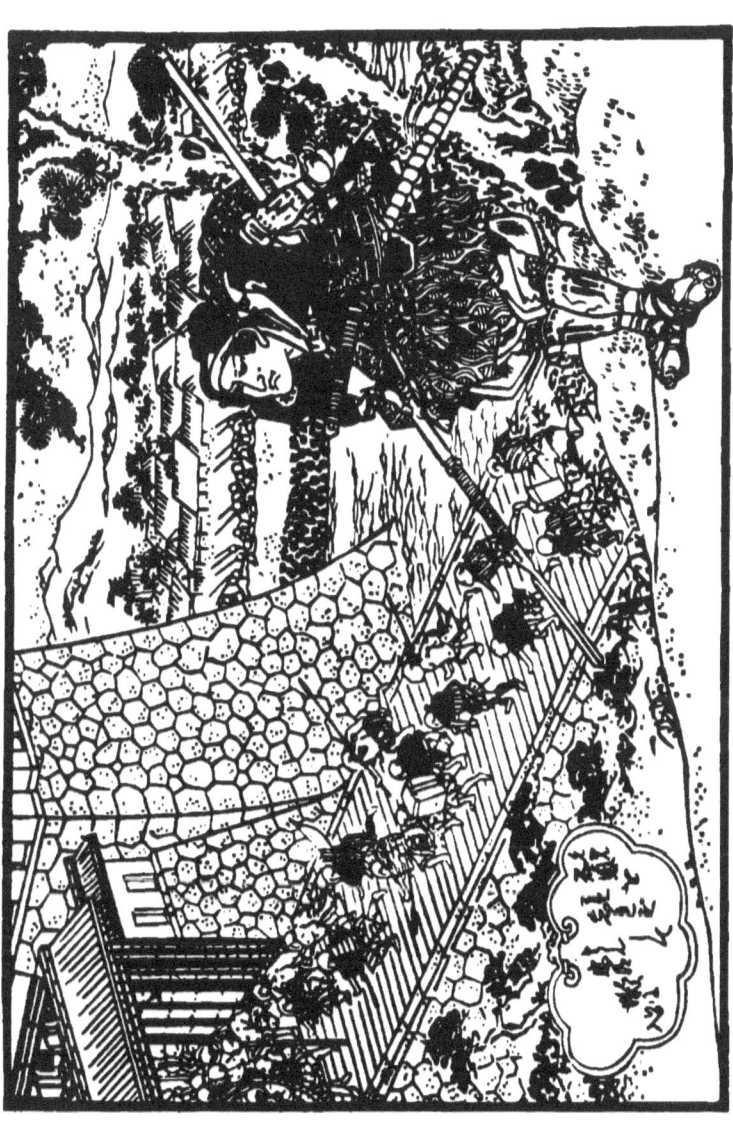

"In the midst of the bustle there appeared a very poorly-clad man, carrying on his back a set of purple armor, and bearing in his hand a formidable spear."

Chap. vi, p. 36.

where he knows there is plenty of rice. He is willing to meet a soldier's death, if he can first of all satisfy the craving of his appetite."

" I do not even give him that much credit," whispered a third. " My opinion is he has heard of those three men whom the chief-councillor supplied with money and clothing and wants to share their good fortune."

" That is it! That is it! " cried the others,

" Yes," said a weazened-faced tailor. " A tramping dog often happens upon a good dinner."

The grim-looking *samurai* did not trouble himself to listen, but, taking his seat upon the stump of a tree near the gate, waited patiently as though expecting a summons from within.

In a few moments an aristocratic, martial-looking *samurai*, named Hatchet, came to the portal and enquired of the registering officers :

" Among those who are waiting for admittance, is there not one—Sir Unconquerable."

The official scanned his list, and bowing respectfully, replied :

" The honorable *samurai* you mention has not yet arrived."

Upon receiving this answer, Sir Hatchet raised his voice and shouted

" Sir Unconquerable! Are you among the crowd? Sir Big-rock is impatient to see you."

" Sir Unconquerable! Sir Unconquerable! " echoed

the officials at the gate ; the cry being taken up by the loungers outside.

On hearing his name called, the saturnine stranger slowly rose and advanced toward the gate, the people falling back as he approached.

Sir Hatchet saluted him with profound respect and said.

" Well met, Sir Unconquerable ! The chief-councillor has been expecting you. Now, Sir, please accompany me to his presence."

Sir Unconquerable turned slowly round and, after glancing contemptuously upon the crowd, followed Sir Hatchet to the council-chamber, leaving the people in amazement ; the tailor presently remarking :

" Great Buddha, we can no longer tell a gentleman by his clothes."

That afternoon when a number of the clansmen were assembled in the council-chamber, talking over their plans and prospects, one of them exclaimed :

" What has become of Sir Island-in-the-front ? He has always been noted for his bravery and loyalty. Surely he has not sought safety in flight. It is now five days since the enrollment began, yet his name does not appear on the lists."

This remark aroused the ire of some young *samurai*, who, clapping their hands to their swords, rose, saying

" We will attend to the matter and pay a visit to Sir Island-in-the-front. If we find him preparing to retire like a crab, we will send him upon a different journey."

Away they went rattling their swords and clattering their clogs, fully determined to carry out their words.

Upon reaching the house they entered without ceremony, and rushing into the reception-room found everything in confusion.

" Ah!" exclaimed their leader. " I knew it ; it is as we expected ; he is in his private apartment. I will be the one to despatch him."

He motioned his companions to remain quiet and advanced to the entrance of the room, when instead of drawing his sword he halted a moment and, pointing forward, said :

" I cannot make this out. There is his armor hanging from the beam ready to be put on at a moment's notice. We have been too hasty."

As he spoke the wife of Sir Island-in-the-front entered from the yard, and falling upon her knees enquired in an agitated voice :

" Honorable sirs, what is your pleasure ?"

To which their leader answered :

" We desire to know whether your husband is preparing to assist in the good work ?"

" Honorable sirs, he is down upon the shore attending to his business."

" Ah!" said the *samurai*. " On the shore is he? Come, gentlemen, we will seek him. After all this looks suspicious."

They swaggered off, three abreast, like stage *dai-mio*, and presently reached the custom-house on the wharf, where they discovered Sir Island-in-the-front busily engaged loading coolies with packages of provisions, on seeing which they rudely demanded what he was about, and why he had not enrolled his name.

The *samurai* listened gravely and replied

" Those packages are destined for the castle. While you have been doubting my loyalty I have been providing the means for your support. That is the reason why I have not had time to enroll my name."

The faces of the young men crimsoned with shame, and, bowing respectfully, their leader said :

" Ten thousand pardons for the ignorance of youth. ' The sparrow cannot comprehend the mind of the eagle.' "

CHAPTER VII.

SEALING THE COMPACT.

" A million evils are not so heavy as a command of the master ;
Balanced against the latter my life is as light as a feather."

These words were uttered by Sir Big-rock upon the
occasion of his receiving an official notification from
the Shogun, commanding him, within thirty days,
quietly and respectfully, to surrender the castle of Ako
to the commissioners who would be despatched for
the purpose of taking possession of the same. This
document reached him about the time Sir Shell and
Sir Pigeon-field arrived in Yedo. However, he did
not communicate its contents to the clansmen, deeming it wisest to await the return of their envoys from
the capital. Meanwhile preparations for the defense were continued and the fortress was victualled to
sustain a long siege.

On the morning of the fourteenth day Sir Shell and
Sir Pigeon-field presented themselves at the gate, and

were immediately conducted to the presence of Sir Big-rock. Their travel-stained costumes and fatigued appearance betokened the severity of their journey.

Sir Pigeon-field being too much exhausted to speak, Sir Shell made the report, which was as follows :

" Sir Chief-councillor, we duly delivered the petition to the proper authorities then made searching enquiry regarding Sir Kira. Alas! Alas! he still lives and though deprived of his office, basks in the sun-shine of the Shogun's favor. We hear his manner is as insolent as ever and that he triumphs in the. disgrace of our house. He has trebled the guards at the gates of his residence and his spies dogged our steps wherever we went. He boasts of the wisdom of Sir Small-grove, his chief councillor, and of the fidelity of his retainers, and laughs at the idea of our avenging the death of our lord. While the latter lies under the shadows of the tall pines of the Spring-Hill cemetery, his enemy gazes at the rising sun, the stately Fuji, and the moon illuminating the Sumida river and mocks the noble spirit. How can the gods permit such injustice ? "

Sir Big-rock listened with deep attention, then replied

" I thank you for your zeal in the discharge of your mission. Please retire and take the refreshment and repose you so greatly need. I desire you will not make known this intelligence to any one, as I wish to think the matter over before I communicate it to the clan."

The messengers bowed and retired, leaving Sir Big-rock to his meditations.

Two days afterward he assembled a second council, and thus addressed its members:

" Fellow clansmen, it is my duty to inform you that the Shogun has commanded me to deliver up the castle to an army of occupation, which, bowing to his authority, I shall do. I have not lightly come to this conclusion. To oppose the lawful authorities would be to dishonor the memory of our late lord, who upon receiving the decree of the Shogun, immediately proceeded to carry out its purport."

The *samurai* listened with grave attention, and when he ceased to speak, looked inquiringly at one another, as though expecting he would say something more; however he remained with his head bowed, whereupon Sir Common said:

" Sir Chief-councillor, while we do not doubt the wisdom of your decision, we hesitate to abide by it without first knowing what is to become of us. Are we to forget our loyalty? Perish the thought!"

The chief-councillor respectfully saluted the speaker, and taking a document from his bosom, said:

" This is my reply!" unfolding the paper and reading, " We, the undersigned, retainers of the Lord of Ako, remembering the countless favors we have received at his hands and those of his ancestors, and the words of the sage ' When the master is insulted, it is for the servant to die,' hereby vow to commit self-de-

spatch and follow his spirit on the Lonely Road, thus
demonstrating to the world our respect for lawful authority and devotion to our chief. If we fail to carry
out this vow, may the vengeance of the hundred million gods of heaven and earth be visited upon us.
January, 1699."

The chief-councillor paused in order to note the effect of his words upon the assembly, then continued :

" To-morrow at the hour of the Horse (noon), we
will re-assemble for the purpose of signing this. The
council is now dismissed."

At the appointed time sixty-three of the clansmen
were kneeling upon the matted floor of the council-
chamber. These men represented the rice separated
from the husks.

After a brief delay Sir Big-rock entered and, saluting them gravely, produced the paper which he un-
folded and reverently deposited on the *tokonoma* in
front of the *sambo.* Turning to the assembly he drew a
little knife from the scabbard of his sword, cut the back
of the third finger of his left hand and placed the bleed-
ing member upon the document, beneath his own
name. He then invited Sir Moat, Sr. to follow him,
but the old *samurai* declined the honor and requested
that the son of the chief-councillor, Sir Big-rock, Jr., a
lad of thirteen, should sign next to his father. The boy
advanced and performed the ceremony, after which the
others, one by one, did the same ; the last to sign
being a foot soldier named Temple-cliff, addressing
whom Sir Big-rock said:

"Your presence here gratifies the spirit of our chief and adds lustre to the reputation of his loyal retainers." Then speaking to the entire assembly, added : "Immediately after the surrender of the castle, we will meet at the family temple of our late lord for the purpose of fulfilling our vow."

The next day Sir Big-rock paid off the paper currency of the clan, and, having set aside a large sum of money for a special purpose, divided the balance left in the treasury among the sixty-three *samurai*, each of whom received twenty-five *rio*.

On the morning of the thirtieth day, the army of occupation arrived before the gate and demanded possession of the fortress, whereupon the chief-councillor ordered Sir Common to marshal the clansmen and march them out of the castle. The occasion afforded an opportunity for the official to display his military knowledge, the manner in which he manœuvred his forces exciting the envy and admiration of the beholders.

The clansmen emerged two abreast from the portal, their arms and accoutrements glistening in the cold sunlight. Crossing the stone causeway they deployed to the right and left and formed into two bodies, one under the command of Sir Common and the other under Sir Unconquerable. They stood motionless, spear in hand, as though ready to obey any order, whether to attack or retire.

While they were thus waiting, Sir Island-in-the-front

quitted the castle, bearing the standard of the late chief. Following him came Sir Big-rock, Jr., clad in ceremonial costume, who carried in his hands the *sambo* covered with the white cloth, the intention being to screen the sacred relic from the profane gaze of the vulgar. Behind him, at a short distance, marched the chief-councillor, guarded by *samurai*, holding in his right hand the key of the main gate.

He waited until his son had joined the body of clansmen under Sir Common, when he despatched a messenger to the commanders of the army of occupation, who advanced with their retinues and received the key, during which ceremony Sir Big-rock and his attendants prostrated themselves upon the ground, while the representatives of the *Sho-gun* were seated upon camp-chairs.

When all was over Sir Big-rock rejoined the clansmen whom he thus addressed :

" The house of Ako no longer exists. I bid you a sorrowful farewell. I trust those among you who may seek new masters will serve them as faithfully as you have served your late lord."

All present bowed low and the clan dispersed.

At the hour of the Horse Sir Big-rock entered the temple of the Snow-clad Pine, bearing reverently in his hand a tablet inscribed with the posthumous name of his lord, behind him being his son carrying the *sambo*. Upon reaching the main hall they were met by the chief priest who received their burdens and deposited them on the altar. The sixty-two were all assembled with their swords placed upon the mats ready for use.

Sir Big-rock advanced to the post of honor and kneeling, prostrated himself; then, without drawing his sword, said :

" The time has not arrived for us to use our weapons upon ourselves, and the reason is to be found in the words of Confucius, ' Thou shalt not live under the same heaven or tread the same earth with the enemy of thy master or thy parent.' The death of our lord must first be avenged. His enemy, knowing full well the spirit that animates us, will render our task a most difficult one, nevertheless we must accomplish it. The king-fisher always finds its prey even though the latter hide at the bottom of the river."

The conspirators listened attentively, and Sir Moat, Sr., replied :

" Sir Big-rock, we will, in all things, be guided by your example and counsel."

The chief priest provided them with paper and other writing materials, upon receiving which their leader wrote a new compact. This the sixty-four sealed with their bloody hands.

From that hour they became in the eyes of men, as they were already in the eyes of the law, *ronin*, owing allegiance to no one but their dead lord.

The clansmen not concerned in the league did

what they considered wisest for the welfare of them-selves and families, the greater number taking ser-vice under a favorite of the Sho-gun, who had lately been created Lord of Sabaye.

Within a week of the surrender of the castle, Sir Big-rock despatched Sir Shell, Sir Cliff-side, Sir Un-conquerable and Sir Thousand-cliffs with other con-spirators to Yedo, instructing them minutely to watch Sir Kira and report his movements, having done which he gave up his residence in Ako and purchased a house in Yamashina, a little town near the city of Kioto.

Upon the death of the Lord of Ako, his wife, Lady Fair-face, assumed the religious name of Pure-gem, and took up her abode in her only possession, a man-sion situated in the Blue Hill district in the western part of Yedo, where, attended by Lady Pine-island and a few faithful maidens, she dwelt secluded from the world, waiting for the time to arrive when the *ronin* would avenge the death of her husband.

CHAPTER VIII.

THE STORY OF A YOUNG WIFE'S SORROW

In the fashionable, northern suburb of Yedo, called
Root-bank, stood a cottage surrounded by beautiful
grounds containing many lovely trees, plants and flowers, which were kept green and fresh by a little stream
that flowed through the domain. The result of an ar-
tistic taste could be seen on every side but, alas, she
who had created the paradise had passed away and
her late home was inhabited by a young bride, who,
only a few months before, had been a famous singing-
girl. At the expiration of her contract she had married a young merchant named Mr. Bright-stone, and
he, proud of his lovely wife, had installed her in that
charming spot. This lady, whose name was Little-
tiger, was left much alone, her husband being absent at
his place of business in the city, and as solitude naturally induces feelings of gloom, she often thought of her
former gay life and contrasted it with the quietness
and stagnation of her new state.

One evening, when the shadows were deepening,

she took up her guitar, which rested against a pillar, and after tuning it, commenced to sing a well-known song.

" As I wandered the Niphon road, alone and sad! my heart beat fast and became as round as the Imon Hill that lay before me.

" Neither the nightingale nor the umbrella man noted the approach of rain, yet my sleeves were wet with showers of tears.

" As the wood vines render the foot of Uyeno Hill difficult to ascend, so is the path of love crossed with thorny obstacles.

" The waters of the Sumida river tranquilly pursue their course, but when my thoughts flow toward my love, I am full of uncertainties."

Instead of completing the song she suddenly laid aside the instrument, and resting her chin upon her hands, said in a musing tone:

" Although my husband will not own it, I am sure, since we have been married, his business has decreased. I believe it is a mistake for any one in his position to disregard public opinion and sacrifice his comfort. Why has he brought me to dwell in such a secluded place? Surely this cannot be the summer-house of which I have heard so much, but one he has hurriedly hired for my reception. He goes off very early to the city and does not return until late at night. The empty state of his money-bag and his worried looks tell the story of his trouble. Though shame and consideration for my feelings, may keep him from imparting the disastrous news to me, I would prefer to learn the worst and share his sorrow, knowing the pangs of un-spoken grief are doubly hard to bear."

The chirping of the birds, calling their mates to their resting-places among the trees, and the dusk of the evening added to her sadness, and tears began to course down her cheeks.

Presently she heard some one opening the gate, upon which she dried her eyes, rose, hurried to the entrance and welcomed her husband, saying :

" Dear Bright-stone, you are very late ? I began to have fears about you."

" Do not be alarmed, Little-tiger; I have been very busy to-day running all over the city and must make another visit before retiring to rest."

He followed her into the house, when his wife, after closing the outer door, knelt close to him and said :

" Dear Bright-stone, please do not go out again this evening; I know not why but something tells me to ask you this; my heart is full of sadness."

He drew her toward him, rested her head upon his knees, and patting her on the back, replied :

" I understand all, Little-tiger. I suppose the con-trast between your gay home and this place is too great. In a few days we will remove to our city residence when I am sure you will feel more cheer-ful."

" Oh, Bright-stone ! " she sobbed. " You do not

understand me. It is not my loneliness but your secret sorrow that renders me so unhappy."

" Little-tiger! Little-tiger !" he exclaimed, " who has been speaking to you about my business affairs?"

" No one," she said. " I have learned all by watching your face. Please do not conceal the nature of your misfortune from me. If I am not worthy to share your trouble, I am unworthy to be your wife."

Her speech greatly affected him and it was some moments ere he could reply, when he said ·

" Dear Little-tiger, your love magnifies your fears. The fact is my business compels me to take a journey, and, truth to tell, I must set out to-night. Now you know all."

" To-night ?" she cried, in a despairing voice. " No, not to-night. Wait until morning."

" I cannot, little one, I must set out at once. Here," withdrawing a package containing five *rio* and a sealed letter from his bosom, " is what I came to bring you. Now I must return to the city. You will here find necessary instructions, and the money will be sufficient to last you until my return."

" Oh, please wait awhile," she cried, clinging to him. " If you must depart this evening, let me accompany you."

" How can I take you where I myself dislike to go. Come, be brave, my Little-tiger."

Her womanly perception penetrated his loving

stratagem, and regarding him with overflowing eyes, she pleaded :

" Oh, my dear husband, sit down again. I understand all. A sudden calamity has overtaken you and you are about to end your life. That letter contains your farewell. Friendless as I am, if I must part from you, I have no need of money. I shall follow the path you take."

She clung to him with one hand and with the other broke the seal of the letter, noticing which he cried :

" My dear, that is not intended for you to read now. I must hurry away."

The agonized wife only grasped him more firmly, as she did so quickly glancing over the epistle, which she presently dropped, exclaiming :

" Ah ! I find it is as I thought. What can I say ? You are blameless. It is I, a woman of low birth, once a singing girl, who has brought this ruin upon you. Still, as you have chosen me for your wife, do you imagine I could survive your death ?"

" No, dear and admirable one," he sobbed, " I have never thought you would be thus unfaithful. Had I done so, I would not have taken pains to provide for you after my death. I know full well the world will brand me as a coward for shirking my responsibilities instead of bravely facing them; but, alas, I have of late been so unfortunate that I am disgusted with my life and am determined to end it. You

quitted your gay circle to please me, and have been
only a prisoner in this wild place, so I thought if I
were out of the way, you would be better off. This
small sum of five *rio* will not go far, still it was obtained honestly, therefore I pray you to accept it."

So saying he sunk down at her feet, prostrated
with grief.

By and by, when she had somewhat comforted him,
she said :

" The gods decree all things for our good. We
will go to the ' Well-of-the-woods' near by, and there
end our lives, dying in the beautiful spot rendered
sacred by the devotion of the singing-girl, White-oak,
who is buried near her lover beneath the spreading
branches of the weeping willow, planted in her memory."

Bright-stone rose, and regarding her tenderly, said :

" The willow tree you mention is said to possess
miraculous power.   Come, we will seek its shelter."

They quitted the house, hand in hand, and proceeded toward the Three-points in the direction of
the " Well-of-the-woods," pausing to pray at the willow tree, to one of the branches of which the wife tied
her silken girdle-string, a sign she had renounced all
hope of life.

As they approached the well they saw the pale
moon reflected upon the placid water, noticing which
they knelt and said their last prayers.   All was lonely
and sorrow-inviting.

After a few moments they rose, joined hands and prepared for the fatal leap when a *samurai* advanced along the path and, divining their intention, rushed forward and seized them.

The new comer was Sir Small-grove, chief councillor of Sir Kira, a man whose loyalty would at any time cause him to cross swords with the enemy of his master, and who, though that master erred, always counselled him rightly, even at the risk of incurring his displeasure.

When Sir Small-grove had drawn them from the edge of the well he enquired the cause of their sorrow, and, upon learning the truth, became greatly interested and did his best to console them, saying :

" My good friends, you are both very young, therefore, doubtless, feel unable to bear such great shame and sorrow. Probably, in your despair, the course you had decided to take appeared the best under the circumstances. It was in truth a very foolish one. There are changes in the career of every man, and though he may fall very low yet who can say he will not rise again. I came here to-night to pray under yonder venerable tree for my honored lord, that the dangers now besetting him may be averted. In being able to save your lives, I recognize a good omen for him. As you have, by my interposition, been delivered from death, so will he be saved from his enemies. I pray you dry your tears and come with me."

Bright-stone and his wife were touched by the kindness of Sir Small-grove, and after gratefully saluting him and returning their thanks, accompanied him to his house where they remained a few days.

It fortunately happened that one Mr. Young-island, an old friend of Sir Small-grove and a mirror-maker by trade, desired to adopt a son, so, at the samurai's suggestion Mr. Bright-stone and his wife were received into the merchant's family.

In a future chapter I will tell how these young people were enabled to return the great kindness rendered them by Sir Small-grove, who, though he served a bad master, was, like Sir Big-rock, a man of a hundred thousand.

Mr. Bright-stone and his wife were touched by the kindness of Sir Small-grove.

Chap. viii. p. 56.

CHAPTER IX.

THE CONTEMPTIBLE BEHAVIOR OF THE TWO COUN-
CILLORS.

" At the first signs of a storm the timid hare seeks safety in the
earth.
When trouble overtakes the master, the disloyal servant fills his
pouch and departs."

I came across this maxim the other day while reading a history of the forty-seven *ronin ;* and as birds
collect various substances with which to form their
nests, so authors search out and use the thoughts of
others, which they weave into their stories. I quote
the foregoing saying in order to illustrate the cases
of those cowardly wretches, Sir Arrow-stand and Sir
Wisteria-lake.

On the night of their lord's death they met in the
apartment of Mrs. White-stocking, wife of Sir Arrow-
stand, and began to talk over their prospects.

" What shall we do ? " nervously enquired Sir
Wisteria-lake, who was the younger of the two men.
" We are blamed for everything that has occurred and
our position has become a very hot one."

" Yes," mournfully answered Sir Arrow-stand, pouring out a big cup of *saki* which he raised to his lips with a shaking hand. " The fact is, Sir Wisteria-lake, we are in a well. Everyone else can go to Ako, but we must seek other and more pleasant quarters. Sir Big-rock will never overlook our blunder. I think the wisest thing for us to do, will be to commit self-despatch and thus secure a good name for the future."

The lady uttered a peculiar sound, indicative of dissent, and resting the palms of her hands upon her knees, gave her husband a significant look, wagging her head as she did so, after the manner of young women mated to old husbands whom they have tamed to wear petticoats.

Sir Arrow-stand, who, though used to that sort of demonstration, was anxious to keep his friend in ignorance of it, gazed at her over his horn-spectacles and mildly remarked :

" Your cough is again troubling you ? "

" I did not cough," she tartly replied. " I said pewgh ! "

Sir Wisteria-lake, who was respectfully waiting for the termination of this domestic encounter, looked enquiringly at Sir Arrow-stand, who he expected would reproach the lady ; however the husband merely replied :

" The noise outside renders conversation somewhat difficult. Honorable wife, what are you condemning? "

" Your determination," she said. " You always forget me. If you commit self-despatch, what am I to do? "

Sir Wisteria-lake bent forward and murmured, as though thinking aloud :

" Follow his honorable example."

Mrs. White-stocking pretended not to hear this remark which, in no manner, agreed with her inclination ; so, after filling and lighting her pipe, she glanced at her husband and said :

" Honorable Sir, listen to me. You and Sir Wisteria-lake have the keys of the treasury, why not accept the benevolent provision of the gods ? To-morrow the commissioners will arrive and pocket all that is left."

Sir Arrow-stand turned to his comrade and remarked in an under-tone :

" The strongest is not always the wisest."

" This is no time to quote poetry," she cried. " If you mean business, go to the treasury at once. I will accompany you and, while you are filling your bags, select some of the soul-stirring robes from my lady's presses ; there are eye-hitters stored there. Now that my mistress is a widow she will no longer have use for such things and, I am sure, would rather know they decorated my back than see them in the possession of the commissioners' favorites."

At first her husband affected to be shocked by her proposition, and Sir Wisteria-lake waved his hand as though signifying he could never consent to such a thing ; however, when they had exhausted their stock

of moral maxims, they took their lanterns and proceeded to the fire-proof building, where the robes and
other treasures of their dead master and living mistress were stored.

The men, who now forgot all scruples, set to work
to fill their bags with *koban* (oval, gold coins of various
values), for which purpose they kicked open the treas-
ure-boxes and otherwise conducted themselves like
burglars.   Sir Wisteria-lake secured the plunder while
Sir Arrow-stand made entries in a note-book, he being
determined, when the time came for them to divide their
prize, his companion should not have more than his share.

This matter kept him very busy, as Sir Wisteria-lake
instead of depositing the *koban* in the common purse, betrayed a tendency to slip them into his sleeve ; therefore
Sir Arrow-stand failed to notice the actions of his wife.

When they were filling the last bag he observed
Mrs. White-stocking on her knees before an immense
bale, which she was securing with a silken cord, while
between her teeth she held a pocket-book, containing
paper-currency, wrapped in a white cloth.   Seeing her
thus employed he said :

" What are you doing ? "

" That is my affair," she mumbled, the pocket-book
preventing her from speaking very plainly.   " Go on
with your business, I will attend to mine."

Hearing this remark Sir Wisteria-lake paused in the
act of placing a *koban* in the bag and said :

" We shall be unable to carry anything so weighty."

"That is my affair," she mumbled.   "Go on with your business.   I will attend to mine!"

" Don't you trouble yourself," she retorted. " I will be my own coolie."

" My dear," whispered her husband, " do not burden yourself with those bulky things ; take money. That will purchase you all the dresses you require."

" Pewgh ! " she contemptuously returned. " There are robes in this bale that cannot be duplicated. When a man meddles with a lady's wardrobe, he attempts something he does not understand."

" As you will, as you will, my dear," he hurriedly replied,

" Yes," she said, leaning back and tightening the cord of the package. " It has been and shall always be as I will."

Sir Arrow-stand uttered a deep sigh and returned to his work. When they had collected as much as they could carry he secured the door of the building and they proceeded toward their house.

Mrs. White-stocking soon dropped her burden and exclaimed :

" It is too heavy ! "

" I told you so," said her husband in a low tone. " Let us hurry ! I do not wish to be discovered in the vicinity of the treasury."

" Not one step will I advance without my bundle," she resolutely answered. " Come, pick it up and carry it between you."

The over-burdened men did as they were required, both being in her power.

They soon reached the house, when she made them pack the money among her movables. An hour before the dawn the party quitted the *yashiki* (mansion), going forth like burglars anxious to avoid the gaze of honest people.

Later on I will describe the punishment that overtook this disloyal trio. Meanwhile we will leave the wretched men to be tormented by the bitter tongue of the shrew.

CHAPTER X.

" The perfect state is only to be obtained by prayer. We will
not kill the birds and will even feed the wild eagles, and by such
deeds shall our lives be rendered pure."

This was the prayer of a pious priest, who many
years ago dwelt in a hermitage on the spot now occupied by the Temple of Asakusa. From that little germ
grew a mighty fabric, which during the prosperous reign
of a wise sovereign, flourished and attracted great
crowds of people, who daily visited it and made their
supplications to the goddess Kuwannon, the mother of
mercy.

The approaches to this beautiful place were lined
with restaurants, among them being a celebrated one
bearing the sign of the Royal Chrysanthemum.

One day, in April, when the cherry-blossoms were
just budding in the Temple gardens, an old, gray-
haired man, accompanied by a beautiful girl of seven-
teen years, entered the inn and took their places on

63

the matted floor of the public room. An attendant quickly placed a screen before them and having obtained their order retired.

The patriarch, whose cheeks were moistened with tears, said to his companion.

" My dear Home, it is not fear that drives me away from Yedo. I am becoming too old to properly take care of you and am afraid that your beauty will prove a source of misery to you. I have therefore made up my mind to quit the city and live in the country. Although you may at first feel lonely and dislike to reside among strangers, you will soon become accustomed to the life. Keep a good heart and bear my decision with patience."

To this explanation and entreaty the maiden affectionately replied :

" Grandfather, as long as you are with me I shall not be friendless, and once in the country no one will annoy us. Still I cannot help feeling regret at having to part with my dear friends and my kind music-teacher."

The old man watched her closely and endeavored to lessen her distress, saying :

" I described our new home as being in the country while in reality Golden-shore is not far from Yedo; it is also a famous watering-place and neither dull nor lonesome. When you desire to see your old friends you can join a party of pilgrims coming hither to pray to the goddess Kuwannon and thus reach the city quite safely."

His words were cheerful, but his heart was sorely troubled at being compelled to take his grand-child from her companions and install her in a strange home, and for awhile he remained silent, absorbed in sad thoughts.

In a short time the quick-footed attendant spread a humble repast before them, and Miss Home was in the act of pouring out *saki* when two strangers swaggered into the room. One of the new comers appeared to be a merchant and the other, a person of rough demeanor, was a middle-man.

Upon seeing the grandfather they advanced to where he was seated, and pushing aside the screen, squatted before him, the middle-man exclaiming :

" Mr. Left-gate-keeper, we have met in a very good place."

The person addressed trembled with apprehension, noticing which his granddaughter glanced uneasily at the intruders whose behavior greatly distressed her.

" Oh, you need not look so very innocent, Mr. Left-gate-keeper," rudely continued the fellow. " To judge from your face, no one would think you knew that your son had borrowed money of this gentleman. You act as though you had a perfect right to take your granddaughter where you please. But, kind Sir, I say you no."

The bewildered grandfather did not reply, simply clasping his hands and regarding the speaker, seeing which the merchant said in a conciliatory tone :

" Mr. Prosperity, have a little patience with him.   I
will take this young girl by way of payment, and thus
wipe out the obligation."

" That is a bright thought of yours," said the middle-
man, and addressing Mr. Left-gate-keeper, he added.
" Do you hear that, Mr. Grandfather, surely it will
satisfy you.   See here, Miss Home, you are to be the
pay for your parent's debt, therefore cannot accompany your relative.   The obligation having been incurred by your father, you will not say no, so come
along with me, at once."

While the men were making ready to start, the
terrified girl turned to her troubled companion and said:

" My dear grandfather, what am I to do?   Is it true
I must accompany these persons?   Can you not help
me?"   Thus speaking she grasped the sleeve of his
robe and began to weep.

Mr. Prosperity laughed heartily and sneeringly
exclaimed :   " Come now, don't give us any more
trouble."

He seized the girl's hands and endeavored to drag
her away, whereupon the old man arose and thrusting
him back, cried :

" What, shall I part with my dear granddaughter
for the paltry sum of five *rio*?   No, no! You shall not
take advantage of my age and the death of my son!
You say he borrowed money of you ; where is your
proof?   Have you his writing to show Whether
you have or not I will, upon reaching Golden-shore,

borrow the amount you demand and forward it to you by a swift messenger. Under no circumstances will I give up the charge of my granddaughter "

" By the sacred mountain ! " ejaculated the merchant. " We are not such fools as to depend upon a mere promise, even though it proceed from the mouth of the old and honorable Mr. Left-gate-keeper."

" Our patience is exhausted," cried the middle-man. " We must and will have this girl."

He once more seized her and dragged her toward the entrance, shouting : " Stop your whimpering and come along."

" Here, man, you go too far," passionately exclaimed the grandparent. " Although I am aged I can still use my sword and will not see my son's daughter kidnapped."

He endeavored to draw his weapon but his palsied hand refused its office, seeing which the merchant retorted :

" Look here, Mr. Left-gate-keeper, I shall not ex-cuse such words."

" Nor I," said the middle-man. " What is the good of your wasting your feeble breath. You know full well you were compelled to leave your house on Buddha-river Street on account of being in arrear with your rent and were not even allowed to remove your furniture. Your promise to pay is a mere trick. We have caught you in the act of running away. You can-not deceive me. Everyone knows what sort of man I am.

My name is Mr. Prosperity and I am termed the back-
bone of the middle-men of Yedo."

As he uttered these bombastic words he glanced
menacingly around at the guests, in order to intimidate
them and prevent their interference, then renewed his
attempt to drag Miss Home from the apartment.

The poor girl, who was almost terrified out of her
senses, broke from him and darted toward a screen
behind which a *ronin-samurai* was seated, partaking
of refreshments. The middle-man pursued her, and in
his struggle kicked over the screen which fell upon the
gentleman, who, enraged at the double outrage, sprang
to his feet and dealt Mr. Prosperity a blow that sent
him upon the floor, then, drawing his sword, stood over
him, exclaiming

" Dog, what do you mean?"

The *samurai* was Sir Shell, who had been refreshing
himself after a tour of inspection, the object of which
was to learn something of the movements of Sir Kira.
He certainly was a handsome young man, and as he
stood there his white complexion, aquiline nose, clear
eyes, rosy lips and brave demeanor, captivated the
heart of Miss Home, who, kneeling by the side of her
grandfather, timidly glanced up at her deliverer.

" You impudent wretch," continued the *samurai*,
" although social distinctions lose their sharpness in a
restaurant, your kicking over my table in the midst of
my dinner is more than I ought to permit. I shall
therefore punish you."

"Your foot kicked over the screen, upon me. I will have that foot."

Both the merchant and the middle-man were greatly frightened and, prostrating themselves with their foreheads to the floor, besought his forgiveness, explaining that they were there to arrest some runaways, in doing which they had not intended to offend the guests, least of all a noble *samurai* like himself.

Sir Shell glanced disdainfully at them and returned :

" I am not about to punish you for your lack of courtesy toward myself, but for your disrespect for age. You men of low degree, taking advantage of this old gentleman's years and helplessness, have sought to kidnap this young lady, in doing which you have violated the laws of your country. Your foot kicked over the screen upon me, I will have that foot."

He drew his sword and flourished it, seeing which the middle-man humbly pleaded :

" Honorable sir, I deserve the punishment, but the noble *samurai* will surely stay his hand when he hears I have a mother and a little son who are entirely dependent upon me for their support."

" Yes, yes," murmured the merchant. " I can vouch for all he says."

Sir Shell deliberated a moment, then observed :

" I should only stain my good sword with the blood of such a reptile. In case I spare you, will you assent to my proposal ? "

" We will agree to anything," they answered. " Name your own conditions."

"Good," he cried. "In the first place you will re-
nounce all claim upon this old gentleman. As for
the sum you demand I will pay that. Under no circumstances will I permit you to interfere with this
young lady;" then turning to Miss Home, he continued "perhaps I am taking too great a liberty—will
you permit me to interfere in this matter?"

The maiden, who felt very bashful in the presence
of the handsome stranger, could only faintly utter :

"I thank you, honorable sir."

Her grandfather came to her aid, saying :

"We are deeply indebted to you. I am really
ashamed to figure in such a disgraceful affair. I shall
regard the money as a loan which I will endeavor
speedily to repay."

Sir Shell bowed and said :

"Honored sir, I beg you not to refer to that, I will
settle this matter."

After which, addressing the prostrate pair, he sternly
said :

"Let me have your decision. Will you take my
money or a thrust of my sword? Ah! I see you prefer the former. Be quick, make out the receipt and be
off."

The exchange was soon made, and in a few moments
the kidnappers were out of the house.

The guests, who had been much alarmed by the
blustering of the intruders, loudly expressed their
admiration for the courage and charity of the *samu-*

rai, while the latter, turning to Mr. Left-gate-keeper, said :

" Honorable sir, you must have felt very anxious , however, thanks to my good sword, the danger has passed from you. Still, even now, you will have to use caution, and it is not safe for you to tarry here. I would advise you to quit the place at once."

The old man bowed profoundly and gratefully replied :

" By some mysterious providence we have received a great charity at your hands." Then, whispering to Miss Home, said : " My dear granddaughter, why do you not thank the honorable gentleman ? "

" Indeed I—I feel under a great obligation to you," she stammered.

" I beg you will not mention it," said Sir Shell. " I know it was discourteous to draw my sword in the presence of so fair a lady, yet the exigency of the case demanded it. I cannot leave you without asking your pardon for my rudeness. I have an urgent duty to perform, therefore must now say farewell. I hope at some future day to be again illuminated by the light of your countenance."

These words caused her heart to beat violently. Poor girl! she was already deeply in love with her gallant rescuer, not because he was young and handsome but on account of his goodness of heart, which had induced him to bestow the large sum of five *rio* upon a passing stranger. His manly generosity touched

her soul, and she felt that to trust her life to such a one
would be like confiding in the gods themselves.   However, being in a public restaurant and unaccustomed to
such places, she was diffident and instead of replying,
whispered something to her grandfather, who, nodding
to her, thus addressed the *samurai* :

" Honorable sir, I desire to make a little explanation.
I have long been annoyed by those men, who had
made up their minds to deprive me of my granddaughter, so I determined to retire to Golden-shore
out of their way.   Now, thanks to your kindness in
getting rid of them, all my plans are in confusion.
May I ask where you reside ? "

The ronin's face flushed slightly, as he evasively
replied :

" Honorable sir, I am bound for Original-place
(the district in which Sir Kira resided).   Why do you
enquire ? "

" Because I desire to return your kindness," whispered Mr. Left-gate-keeper.   " This is no place for
conversation and I—I—I was about to say—"

Instead of completing his speech he paused and
glanced downward with a puzzled air, on which the
young lady sighed and said :

" Would it were possible always to remain in the
place of one's birth. "

Sir Shell, comprehending her meaning, urged her
relative to return to the city, to which the old man
agreed.

This decision so delighted Miss Home that, forgetting her bashfulness, she exclaimed :

" Oh! great happiness, then we shall travel the same road as this gentleman. Our home is in the district of Original-place,"

Such incidents as these teach us the mysterious ways and workings of the gods who preside over the tying of the thread of love.

CHAPTER XI.

THE OLD, OLD STORY.

"Who can oppose the will of the god of Izumo (fate). Even the great warrior is conquered by love."

Sir Shell, Mr. Left-gate-keeper and Miss Home quitted the restaurant together and the young people were so delighted with each other's society, that the distance between the Temple-grounds and Original-place appeared but a few paces.

By the time they reached Buddha-river Street the sun had sunk below the horizon and the shadows of the evening were gathering over the city.

Mr. Left-gate-keeper called upon his landlord, who dwelt near by, and after paying the arrears of rent, received a new lease of his old home, whereupon he invited Sir Shell to enter it and partake of a cup of *saki*. How simple are the ways of the poor!

It was too late for Sir Shell to call upon his friend, Sir Unconquerable, who wished to consult him with regard to a despatch received from Sir Big-rock, so accepting the pressing invitations of Miss Home and her

grandparent, he remained as their guest, fully intend-
ing to leave early the next morning.

At daybreak he drew aside the paper-screen and
glanced out, when he saw the rain descending in a
perfect deluge from the leaden sky. The down-pour
continued, finding which he made it an excuse and
spent the whole day listening to the charming voice of
Miss Home, who delighted him with songs and her
spirited performance upon the guitar.

While the young lady was preparing the evening
meal he looked round the house and noticed the
poverty-stricken appearance of the apartments, it being
plain enough to him that the inmates would be at a loss
to procure even the next day's rice. He entered the
kitchen, took two *rio* from his purse, presented them
to Miss Home and said :

" This is a very small amount but I pray you to accept
it and expend the money in purchasing some delicacies
for your venerable grandfather. He has few years to
live and it is every one's duty to make him happy."

As he was speaking Mr. Left-gate-keeper came
from an adjoining room and, bowing low, said :

" Those who remember the aged will themselves
attain the honorable years."

This remark pleased Sir Shell, and after they had
chatted for awhile, he said :

" Pardon the question I am about to ask. Have you
any occupation ? If one lives without earning, even a
mountain-high fortune will soon be spent."

" The landlord, who took a fatherly interest in the orphan, patted her on the shoulder and whispered words of consolation."

seized with a fit. I heard him moaning and upon going to his aid discovered he was speechless."

The *ronin* arose and accompanied her to the miserable apartment, on the floor of which lay Mr. Leftgate-keeper, whose features were ashy with the pallor of death.

He glanced up at the young man, then, closing his eyes, gave a gentle sigh, and the thread of his existence was snapped in twain.

Sir Shell and the young lady knelt by the body until the morning light illuminated the placid face of the dead, when Miss Home summoned the neighbors, to whom she sorrowfully communicated her bereavement.

In a short time the corpse was prepared for burial, and as the smoke of the burning incense circled about the apartment, the poor girl knelt and wept—the women present uniting their lamentations with hers and exclaiming :

" Alas ! alas ! the venerable man is no more."

Sir Shell, who looked on sorrowfully, could not find it in his heart to abandon Miss Home in her hour of trouble, and the landlord, who took a fatherly interest in the orphan, patted her on the shoulder and whispered words of consolation.

Now her relative was dead all seemed to look upon Sir Shell as her guardian or brother.

The young man gave full scope to his generosity and not only saw the dead properly buried, but pro-

vided the neighbors with funeral gifts, in fact, treated
them with so much respect and attention that they
would not permit him to depart for three or four days.

On the fifth morning he informed Miss Home he
must start early on the following day, after which, he
busied himself with certain transactions, which through
the helplessness of the young girl, devolved upon
him.

As the shades of evening deepened and the hum of
the city grew faint, Miss Home sat in the veranda and
watched the fire-flies flitting through the tall grass.
These, as they came and went, seemed to her like the
spirits of her departed friends.   Her thoughts were
full of sadness and her tears flowed freely.   A few
months before she had lost her father ; now her grandparent and only relative was gone, her future was
full of uncertainty ; how could she support herself?
The man to whom she had in secret given her heart,
was indeed kind, but his was the devotion of a brother.
During their five days of almost constant companion-
ship no word had fallen from his lips which she could
interpret otherwise than as the utterance of pure friendship.   If she allowed that opportunity to pass without letting him know the state of her heart, he might
never learn the truth.   She had heard the neighbors
whisper :

" In the midst of her affliction Miss Home has found
happiness.   She is really to be envied.   She and Sir
Shell will make a handsome couple."

These reflections inspired her with both joy and sorrow. Joy that any one should think she had found favor in the eyes of him whom she so loved, and sorrow for fear he merely pitied her and that congratulations might be turned to sneers.

She made up her mind if he went away without expressing affection for her, to follow her grandfather.

Thus thinking, she hid her face in the sleeves of her garment and sobbed bitterly. Her grief quickly attracted the attention of Sir Shell, who, coming to her assistance, tenderly conducted her indoors, placed her by the fire-bowl and, seating himself near by, said :

" My dear Miss Home, what is troubling you ? You must not grieve so much for the loss of your relative. The gods are good and, though they do not restore our friends, give us new ones."

The agitated girl sobbed on and, glancing downward, replied :

" When you are gone, who will be left to care for me ? "

She paused and not a sound was heard but the beating of their hearts.

Presently some crows, roosting in the trees surrounding the dwelling, began to cry to the moon, hearing which Sir Shell said :

" The bird of love makes me feel bold. Dear and beautiful Miss Home, I would wish ever to be near you. Can you look with favor upon an unfortunate *ronin ?* "

Her reply was drowned by the voices of the birds, while the moon, peeping through the open window, revealed the beautiful scene. She knelt with her head bent, hiding her blushing face and exhibiting only her snow-white neck, with her taper fingers interlaced on her lap, looking more charming than the half-opened bud of a chrysanthemum.

" Sir Shell—Sir Shell—will your loyalty prove greater than your love for your dainty bride ? "

CHAPTER XII.

SIR KIRA.

" He who has committed a great wrong hears in the scampering
of a mouse the footsteps of the avenger.
No sound alarms the placid soul of the well-doer.

This accurately describes the feelings ot Sir Kira,
who, dreading the vengeance of the loyal *ronin*, hid
himself in his private apartments and, like a bat, only
went out at night.

A more miserable existence could scarcely be imagined—his enormous wealth yielded him no happiness, his suspicious soul feared a traitoress in each of
his beautiful attendants, he trusted no one but his
chief-councillor, Sir Small-grove, and while waiting for
the just retribution he knew must sooner or later follow
his crime, died a thousand deaths. His residence was
guarded not only by his own retainers, but by a body
of men belonging to his son, Lord Uyesugi, spite of
which he would start at the slightest noise and worry

his people by complaining of their negligence and disregard for his safety.

Instead of feeling regret he took comfort in the fact
that Lord Morning-field was dead. He spent his days
in sending out spies to watch the man whom he most
feared, Sir Big-rock, and in consulting with his friends
how to bring his political influence to bear against the
scattered members of the clan of Ako. His bitter
hatred extended even to the innocent widow, Lady
Pure-gem, whom he surrounded with detectives and
watched as a tiger does his prey.

When the autumnal flowers were blooming in the
gardens of his residence, a messenger arrived post-
haste from Kioto, on hearing which Sir Kira directed
his attendants to conduct the man to his presence
and thus addressed him :

" I hope you have brought me good news ? "

The kneeling retainer raised his head and murmured:

" My lord, the information I have is for your ear
alone."

Sir. Kira motioned his servants to retire and bidding the messenger approach close to him, said :

" Now speak."

" My lord, your instructions have been fully carried
out. My wife, Convolvulus, is installed in the house
of Big-rock as an attendant upon his children, my
brother is in his employ as gate-keeper, and five of
your loyal retainers are living within bow-shot of his
dwelling."

" Yes, yes!" impatiently remarked Sir Kira.
" What is the news ? "

" My lord, I have learned this much. A week before I left Kioto, Big-rock received a communication
from the Council of Elders. Their letter evidently
caused him great annoyance. I, therefore, instructed
my wife to ascertain its contents. This proved a very
difficult matter; however, by dint of using caution, she
succeeded in getting a sight of the document."

" Well, well ! " testily exclaimed Sir Kira. " What
was in it ? "

" The council neither granted nor denied the prayer
of the petitioners for the restoration of the clan, and
at the same time gave Big-rock plainly to understand
if he made any attempt to avenge the death of his
lord, both he and whoever joined him would experience the full power of the law. That night he went
to the house of Hatchet, where he met a number of
other *ronin*. The notification from the council was evidently a death-blow to their hopes. They emptied many
bottles of *saki* and sent to a neighboring restaurant
for refreshments. I was hanging round the spot, and
bribed one of the waiters to let me take his place, and
thus obtained admission to the house. Said Big-rock
' This news is a skull-cracker. I have made up my
mind what to do. The honorable Sir Kira has the
best of the game. It is useless for us to worry about
reëstablishing the clan. Each must look out for
himself. As for me, for many years I have worked '

hard, so, in future, intend to enjoy my life.   What say you, Hatchet?'

"The poet replied very indignantly, and the other *ronin* joined him, whereupon Big-rock took the bottle, and filling a cup, remarked : ' *Saki* is the medicine for all diseases.'

"The next day Big-rock was drunk, and he has not since been sober.   Now, my lord, have no apprehension.   Without their leader the clansmen can do nothing ; they will be like a flock of geese that has lost its pilot."

Sir Kira thought for a while, then summoning Sir Small-grove, bade the man repeat the story, after which he said :

"What think you, Sir Councillor?"

"My lord, this news astounds me.   We must continue to watch our enemy."

"Yes, we will not relax our vigilance.   Let the messenger return and take with him some young men in my service, whom you will instruct to follow Big-rock closely, and, if possible, engage him in a quarrel that will result in his no longer being able to trouble us."

The next day a number of Sir Kira's retainers started for Kioto, and, from that time, Sir Big-rock was surrounded by an army of spies, who reported everything he did to their anxious employer.

CHAPTER XIII.

SIR BIG-ROCK DIVORCES HIMSELF.

" The hunted badger shams death.
" With an unscrupulous enemy, even a nobleman has to resort to trickery."

Sir Big-rock, having always been famous for his virtues, astonished the world when he gave himself up to drunkenness and dissipation, yet, though his neighbors shook their heads and secretly condemned his conduct, his good wife uttered no word of reproach, and neither by look nor action showed her sorrow and amazement.

One morning in December, after he had been absent from home all night, she saw him staggering up the pathway, noticing which she hurriedly sent her two little children into her private apartment, being anxious they should not see their father in such a disgraceful state.

Sir Big-rock entered the house with his clogs on, and sinking upon the floor, said to her :

" I want some *saké*."

She replied as though he had treated her with the greatest politeness, and bringing him a cup of the best, knelt by his side and presented the liquor, saying :

" My honorable husband, you are fatigued　Shall I prepare a bed for you ? "

He took a sip of the liquid, and throwing the rest upon the matted floor, drowsily answered :

" Is that the sort of stuff you give me ? "

" My dear husband, it is the finest *saké* in Kioto. You are tired with your journey and everything tastes badly !"

" Journey, journey?　I have only been to the tea-house on Gi-on Street."

Just then some of the servants entered, seeing whom the lady said in a low tone :

" Do not disturb your master, he is not well.　Fetch a pillow for his head."

Sir Big-rock, who appeared to fall into a deep sleep, permitted them to arrange a bed for him, after which his wife knelt by his side, fearing his head would slip from its support and that he would lie uncomfortably. As she watched him, she unconsciously gave vent to her thoughts, little imagining he heard what she said.

" I am an unhappy woman.　Evidently I have been remiss in my duty, else why does my husband turn from me and seek the society of others.　Alas! alas! I fear the death of our lord has disturbed the beautiful balance of Sir Big-rock's mind.　He, who used to be so just, so kind and thoughtful, has of·late strangely found fault and blamed me tor what I have not done. Still I think I must have been negligent in some way, though I cannot remember in what. When he sobers I will respectfully ask him how I have offended, as I can no longer bear this terrible agony. Better die than incur the displeasure of my husband. I will leave him and see that his bath is ready. Ah me! the happy days of the past when he thought his wife was without fault."

The poor lady conquered her sobs, and drying her eyes, softly retired, as she did so, regarding the sleeping man with the utmost tenderness.

When she was well out of hearing, Sir Big-rock arose with no trace of intoxication in his manner, but with features expressive of the deepest agitation.

" Ye gods!" he moaned. " How faithful she is! I cannot bear this!"

As he spoke the tears trickled down his cheeks.

" She is a model of a wife. Instead of blaming me for what would appear to be a crime on my part, she invents thousands of excuses for my conduct and takes upon herself all the odium. I will end this at once. She shall not witness the scenes I must enact in order to carry out my plan of deceiving Sir Kira. Then again my little children shall not remember me as a drunken sot. I will put her away; yet how can I do it?"

This brave, strong man paced the floor, grasped his arms and clenched his teeth in his agony. Wise as he was, he had, in undertaking to play the role of a dissolute man, forgotten how impossible it would be to overcome the devotion of his wife. The only thing left to him was to give her a letter of divorce and send her, with their younger offspring, to his father-in-law, who he knew would understand the true reason for his act and afford her comfort and advice.

Presently he heard the sound of his children's voices, and his wife saying in a low tone

" Do not make a noise, my little ones. Papa is not well, you will disturb him."

" Has he got that funny sickness again ? " demanded the elder boy.

" Hush! hush! " said the mother. " Papa has many troubles and you must not speak thus."

The unhappy man thought of his duty to his dead lord, and, steeling himself against all else, returned to his bed and once more pretended to slumber.

About noon his wife entered and kneeling beside him, waited until he opened his eyes, when she said :

" Honorable husband, your bath is ready."

" Bath ? " he exclaimed, rising and taking a flageolet from its rest. " I am going out."

He moved in the direction of the door, seeing which she picked up his *ronin* hat and kneeling presented it to him, saying :

" Honorable husband, I pray you to put this on. You have enemies about."

Sir Big-rock turned toward her and said :

" Honorable husband, I pray you to put this on. You have enemies about."

Chap. xiii, p. 88.

CHAPTER XIV

THE STORY OF DOCTOR BUTTERFLY-COTTAGE.

"Some soldiers accomplish great military deeds while running
away from the enemy.
The ignorant attempts of quacks occasionally result in good
consequences."

No one is more to be pitied than he who places his
life in the hands of a quack. Unfortunately many
such foolish persons exist, because, throughout all
ages, people have been more inclined to listen to
rogues than to follow the advice of honest men.
Must we not be cautious ?

There are many mock-doctors to be found everywhere. These fellows, utterly ignorant of the science
of medicine, which the ancients so closely studied and
reduced to a system, pretend to cure diseases of which
they do not even know the names, and entrapping
their victims by a great show of books and scientific
instruments, by threats and deceit, compel them to
swallow the most nauseating compounds.

If, once in a while, they make a hit, the whole country rings with their praise, and they walk the earth with their heads in the clouds.

The ancient professors of medicine established certain rules which are followed to this day. They first ascertained the comparative value of drugs, then mixed them in specified proportions, taking care that the effects of one ingredient should counterbalance the others, and thus produce a harmonious result. A patient suffering from fever requires medicines containing *in* (cold) properties, and one shivering with a chill should be dosed with *yo* (hot) drugs, to equalize the temperature of the system. However, a person afflicted with fever must not take only cold-producing physic, or the one who has a chill be treated with drugs that merely create heat. A skilful physician gives certain quantities of each remedy, in addition to which he uses acupuncture and the moxa. In the foregoing consists the science of medicine, which is only acquired by long study and serving a number of years as assistant to a regular practitioner. Some drugs ought to be administered in their natural state, others require careful preparation, or their effects prove very injurious to the patient. Now a quack, not having studied these principles, blindly administers his nostrums, trusting to the god of luck to carry him through. If his patient dies, he solemnly shakes his shaven head and says to the weeping relatives :

" I was sure of this from the beginning."

Beware of quacks! they live upon the weakness of

The snow was falling lightly, and he protected his shaven
head with a paper umbrella.

Chap. xiv, p. 93.

answered all inquiries, and, by his important air, added greatly to the respectability of his master. Once inside the yard the visitor noticed a tablet, inscribed as follows:

" Those who require to be examined are requested to come before the hour of the Snake (10 A. M.), not later

" We refuse to visit patients living any great distance from our residence."

This was intended to impress his clients with an idea that he had more business than he could attend to.

Thus lived Dr. Butterfly-cottage, physician to Sir Kira, who was, in his day, the greatest quack in the metropolis.

One morning in February, 1700, this worthy approached the rear gate of his house, carrying in his hand a horse-mackerel, wrapped about with rushes. The snow was falling lightly and he protected his shaven head with a paper umbrella, while his feet were kept from the wet by high clogs. Under ordinary circumstances the doctor would not have been seen bearing his own dinner; however, his old bohemian taste sometimes returned and led him to do things incompatible with his new dignity. He was the brother of the cowardly renegade, Sir Arrow-stand, and, like him, crafty, treacherous and over-reaching. When quite a young man he had behaved so badly that he incurred the disfavor of the Lord of Ako, who, notwithstanding

Sir Arrow-stand's pleading, banished him from the Province of Harima. Being but imperfectly educated, he was at his wits' end how to obtain a living, and for some years wandered aimlessly about the country, finally drifting to Yedo where he established himself as a go-between in marriages, and real-estate agent. By-and-by, he contrived to creep into the good graces of Sir Kira, whom he cured of a trifling, though painful ailment. After accomplishing this feat he set up as a physician, and by dint of making great display, and through the influence of his patron, soon became well known. His library was the talk of the neighborhood, his collection of medical appliances was mysterious and appalling, and his furniture and ornaments were unique and elegant, notwithstanding which he could neither read nor write. His only stock in trade was his ready wit and a thorough knowledge of human nature.

As he entered the house he handed his burden to his kneeling servant, saying :

" Tell the cook to prepare that for my mid-day meal. I wish it stewed with leeks. Bring me a cup of hot *sake*, I feel the cold principle predominating in my body."

The man hastened to obey, and the doctor, after casting aside his heavy outer garment and unwinding the white silk wrap from about his throat, crouched over the *hibachi* (fire box), and warmed his chilled fingers.

The attendant soon returned with the tray on which

were a kettle of hot *saké* and a cup. Kneeling by his
master he served him, saying :

" There is a man from the Blue-hill district waiting
to see you."

" He is early," said the doctor, holding out his cup
for more *saké*. " Tell him I am very busy studying a
case and will see him presently. I must smoke a few
pipes before I can receive patients. People should
not expect a doctor to wait on them at once like a
store-keeper."

After he had refreshed himself and taken a bath, the
visitor was ushered into his presence. The new-comer
was dressed in the costume of a merchant in easy circumstances, and had a simple, polite manner which fav-
orably impressed the doctor, who, responding to his
salutation, blandly observed

" You are the gentleman from the Blue-hill district,
are you not ? "

" I have the pleasure of seeing you for the first
time," said the man. " I am from the place you name,
and have come to consult you concerning a relative of
mine, who is employed in an apothecary store on Main
Street. Of late, he has been much disturbed in his
mind, and talks the wildest nonsense. I would like
you to prescribe for him. Your fame has been noised
all over the city."

Dr. Butterfly-cottage simpered like a vain woman
who is complimented, and replied :

" Under ordinary circumstances I could not take a

new patient, still as you have come from such a distance, I will see your relative ; besides, the treatment
of crazy people is my specialty. But there is something I have to tell every new-comer. Doctors re-
semble dried fishes ; you cannot know their quality
by looking at them. Then again, you remember the
saying, ' the pay of a physician is like the cherry-
blossoms on the high mountain, it cannot be reached '
(literally demanded). That is why definite prices
have been fixed for certain kinds of medicine. We,
of our honorable profession, being prevented from demanding recompense for our advice, have to com-
pensate ourselves by charging for drugs. I will not
be strict with you and exact payment in advance,
though I must have an understanding concerning my
fees. This is my invariable practice, yet I find it does
not decrease the number of my patients. I com-
mence mixing early in the morning and begin my
rounds after mid-day, often not returning until late at
night. My great reputation and large practice excite
the envy and hatred of all my brother practitioners,
who maliciously term me the ' scavenger doctor.' Is
it not ridiculous ? Now you understand my way of
doing business. If you wish to engage me I am at
your service."

His visitor bowed low and replied :

" Honorable doctor, if you will undertake my relative's case, I care not how much I have to pay you.
I am even ready to give a sum in advance, only I
must first be assured you can cure him."

" Cure him, cure him ! " ejaculated the quack, clapping his hands together. " Honorable sir, I always cure my patients. The illustrious nobleman, Sir Kira, who is in such favor with the Sho-gun, calls me Doctor Never-fail. When I have clients who appreciate me, I do my best, which means cure. Tell me the symptoms of your friend's disease."

" Honorable doctor, he is crazy. Imagines all manner of things."

" Yes, yes," patronizingly interposed the other. " Those are the symptoms described in the ancient books on lunacy. Of course he thinks himself somebody else and believes he is pursued by enemies ?"

" Not exactly," quietly answered the man. " My relative's illusion is a very peculiar one. He is continually saying : ' I would like to have the money for the pearls.' "

" Ah ! I will soon cure him of that. Suppose we say five *rio* for my attendance and medicine during the period of ten days. Will that be satisfactory to you ? "

The simple one bowed and murmured :

" I would not care if it were a little more."

" Well, then, give me six *rio*."

The man produced his purse, and handing the sum to the doctor, remarked

" Honorable sir, I will bring the patient early tomorrow. Please do not be harsh with him. Remember he will say, ' I would like to have the money for the pearls.' "

When the visitor had departed, the doctor glee-
fully polished his shaven pate with his right hand, and
after chuckling awhile, cried :

" Gracious me! that customer does not appear to
know what avariciousness is. Unless I add some new
patients to my list I shall be compelled to give up my
norimono. I must fill the gaps caused by my little
mishaps. I have earned six *rio* of his money and will
keep him paying as long as he has a coin in his
pouch."

While he was rejoicing, the clock on the *tokonoma*
struck the hour of the Horse (mid-day).

The next morning the merchant presented himself
at a celebrated drug store on Main Street, and handing a letter to the proprietor, boldly remarked :

" Will you please attend to this matter at once ? "

The druggist opened the communication, and after
reading it, said :

" This is from Dr. Butterfly-cottage. I see he requires a number of pearls of the very best quality.
One of my people shall pick them out and take them
round to Gold-mountain Street."

" I will wait and accompany him," said the messenger.

He walked around the place as though it belonged
to him, and after the clerk had the pearls ready, observed :

" You must go quickly. The doctor is anxiously
awaiting my return."

"The man bowed and when the merchant turned to enter the inner apartment, derisively stuck out his tongue."

Chap. xiv, p. 99.

Upon arriving at the house, the merchant stepped into the reception room, and addressing the clerk, who stood respectfully in the entrance, said :

" Give me the package and remain here until you are summoned. The doctor wishes to send some things back to your master."

The man bowed, but when the merchant turned to enter the inner apartment, derisively stuck out his tongue, then laughingly exclaimed :

" That fellow, although he looks simple, talks very big! I suppose he thinks because he is in the service of this quack he has a right to put on airs."

He waited in the ante-room for some time, the proprietor of the house being unusually busy with patients. At last an attendant came out and said :

" Are you the young man from the apothecary on Main Street? "

" Yes, sir, I am."

" Then follow me."

When Dr. Butterfly-cottage saw him, he enquired :

" Well, sir, how do you find yourself to-day? "

" Quite well, doctor."

" Quite well, eh? Come into my private office and let me examine you."

The clerk, though not comprehending his meaning, did as he was requested. To his amazement, the doctor felt his pulse, saying :

" Ah! I knew it, the hot principle predominates. Now your tongue? "

placed his hands upon his knees, and, making a mock obeisance, cried

" Will you pay me for those pearls? I don't care what you call me, as long as you hand me over the money. It is not I who am out of my senses."

" Young man," sternly returned the doctor, "there is no end to your tongue. I am not accustomed to be addressed in such a disrespectful manner Cease your clamor. Your demanding payment for pearls I have never received is calculated to throw a blemish upon my honorable face. Being a person of the highest respectability, I can afford to treat such a charge with the contempt it deserves, still I do not intend you shall rush about the city with your mouth full of such accusations. I will have you secured until I can communicate with your relative."

Upon hearing this the clerk produced the order from his bosom, remarking in a satirical voice :

" Will you deny your own writing ? Here is a note signed by yourself, ordering a number of pearls of the best quality. Perhaps this is a symptom of my sickness ? "

Doctor Butterfly-cottage took the letter, which he held upside down and regarded with blank amazement.

" Is not that your signature ?" cried the man. " Turn it the right way and look at it."

The doctor reversed the paper, and being unwilling to acknowledge his ignorance of reading and writing, said, in a bewildered manner :

" Yes, I always sign my orders thus—though I do not remember issuing this one."

" At last we are beginning to arrive at an understanding," said the clerk. " Of course, as that document is correct, you will pay me for the pearls? "

A few moments calm talk convinced both parties they had been swindled by an adventurer. When the clerk returned to his master, the latter insisted upon receiving his due ; saying, as the doctor had written the order, he must be held responsible. Finally, the quack paid the large sum demanded, (six hundred *rio*) preferring to lose his gold rather than acknowledge his profound ignorance. Although he did his utmost to keep the affair quiet, it gradually leaked out, and soon the song sellers on the streets were heard chanting a poem that made flushes of shame glow through the thick skin of the doctor's face.

CHAPTER XV

The reader will remember that soon after the surrender of the castle of Akó, Sir Big-rock despatched
certain of the conspirators to Yedo, with instructions to watch Sir Kira and report his movements.
Among these loyal men was Sir Cliff-side, who had a
most extraordinary adventure, which I will now relate.

This *samurai*, like his companions, had been very
diligent, never heeding what fatigue he underwent.
For twenty months he traveled all over the city and
suffered the extremes of heat and cold, finally contrac-
ting a disease that rendered him partially blind and
confined him to his home, a small house far from any
other dwelling, in the part of Yedo called Preaching-
court, in the district of Made-land. Here he resided
with his servant, Original-help, who, in the month of
February, 1700, had unexpectedly presented himself,
saying :

"Honorable master, the news of your sickness has

reached Ako. I have come to nurse and attend upon
you."

Sir Cliff-side was over-joyed and placed himself
entirely in the faithful man's hands. During eight
months Original-help tended him day and night, and
watched him with the greatest solicitude.

Toward the end of autumn when the leaves were
red, the sick man began to show signs of improve-
ment and would sit for hours in the little veranda,
watching the ships going and coming on the blue
waters of the bay. One afternoon as he was thus
employed, the cackling of a flock of geese passing
overhead brought to his memory thoughts of the
home where he had left his wife and children.

"Ah!" he sighed. "Who would not feel sad to
hear that sound There go the winged messengers,
yet they have brought no news to me. I have, since
spring, been sick, helpless and unable to do my duty,
like Sir Shell and the rest. I fear I shall leak out of
the conspiracy. Although I have constantly and fervently prayed to the god of medicine, he has been
slow to hear me, added to which this prolonged suspense with regard to Sir Big-rock's plans and my lack
of funds, have rendered me doubly miserable."

He sat for some time in a deep reverie, watching
the receding line of geese until it vanished upon the
horizon, when he was aroused by Original-help saying:

"My honorable master, at last your medicine is
ready, please take it while it is hot. The days are

Sir Cliff-side, pointing in the direction, replied :
" Yes, he is pulling the line from the water."

getting so short I could not have it prepared earlier. I had no idea it was such a great distance to Yeast Street. Doctor Original-course was absent attending our lady. When he returned he told me she had inquired most kindly after you."

"That was very good of her," said Sir Cliff-side. "Though my trouble has been hard to bear, it is, when compared with hers, as light as down. The gods give her comfort and hasten the day when we can look at the sun without blushing."

Original-help knelt by his side and poured some of the hot medicine from a pot into the cup, saying :

"Honorable master, I think your eyes look better."

"Yes, I can see yonder mountains of Kazusa, and Awa, and the sails far away down on the bay."

"Indeed, indeed! The gods be praised, you will soon be quite well again. Can you discern that boat next to the fishing craft, the one in which a man is tending a net ? "

Sir Cliff-side pointing in the indicated direction, replied :

"Yes, he is pulling the line from the water. See he grasps the buoy of the net. He is taking out a fish. What a large one, how it struggles!"

"My honorable master, you are all right. You must thank Dr. Original-course. He seems to understand your constitution."

"That he does. He is a most skilful physician. He treated me when I was a boy at Ako, and our late lord highly esteemed him. He is a very different man from Doctor Butterfly-cottage. Have you ever heard of that knave?"

"Yes, my honorable master, I once had occasion to consult him."

"How foolish of you. He is an unscruplous pretender. Of how much did he rob you?"

Original-help cast down his eyes and respectfully answered

"Honorable master, there are some things to which we do not like to refer. I promise you I will never go near him again. Dear me, it is growing dusk and you will not be able to see, I must get the light ready."

He rose and quitting the veranda, went in-doors, leaving his master to watch the setting sun, which presently sank below the horizon. Then the color of the water changed from blue to black, the angry wind began to whistle and the scene, lately so enjoyable, became sad and gloomy. Sir Cliff-side followed his servant and seating himself by the *tokonoma*, on which stood his sword-rack, covered with a cloth, lighted his pipe and resumed his meditation.

When the shadows had deepened into night he was aroused by voices outside, and some one demanding:

"I beg your pardon. Does Sir Cliff-side live here?"

Original-help being engaged in the attic, Sir Cliff-side answered the summons, saying:

"Yes, I am here. Who might you be?"

"What, my honored master, is that yourself! I am

so glad. It is I, Original-help, who have traveled all the way from Ako as escort to your honorable wife."

The speaker then turned to some one who was with him and said :

" Come, the honorable wife, this is the temporary residence of my master. Young master-babies, you will now see your father."

Sir Cliff-side was both puzzled and surprised ; puzzled at the strange speech of Original-help and surprised at the sudden arrival of his wife and children.

" Mamma, mamma, please untie my sandals. I want to go in quickly," cried the elder boy. " Papa, papa, it is I, your little son, New-six. Brother Help-of-six is with us."

"Come in ! come in," joyfully answered Sir Cliff-side. " I cannot rise to welcome you, as I am suffering from a sickness called bird's-eye, and am unable to see anything in the twilight. Welcome, Bamboo, my wife! So you have arrived from home. Lave your feet and enter at once. Original-help will furnish you with water and towels. If I try to move I shall fall over something. How pleased I am! Be quick, send the children to me and come yourself."

"I wonder where the buckets are kept," said Original-help, stumbling about in the entry. " Wait a moment. I will use my flint and steel."

When the servant had lighted a candle, Bamboo surveyed the place and noted its miserable appointments. The mats covering the floor were old and full of holes, there were great rents in the paper-screens through which came strong draughts, the plastering on the walls was cracked in all directions, and the only handsome article of furniture was the *katanakake* (sword-rack) which stood on the *tokonoma* and held Sir Cliff-side's weapons.

"My honorable husband, are your eyes still bad?" she remarked, as she hastily made her toilet. "I was most anxious to know how you were, so as we came through the city, called upon Dr. Original-course. He told me you would soon be quite well."

"Yes, that is correct. I don't mind my sickness now you and the little ones have arrived."

She entered the room, knelt before Sir Cliff-side, placed her hands on the floor, and bending her forehead to the mat, respectfully saluted him, saying :

"My honorable husband, I have not seen you for many, many months, during which time I have been longing to look once more upon your face. You must have lived very uncomfortably in this wretched habitation. Who has attended upon you?"

"Original-help," said Sir Cliff-side. "He is as industrious and kind as ever."

"I understand, my honorable husband, you have a servant whom you call Original-help, after the faithful man who has escorted me from home."

"Escorted you from home, Bamboo? Why he has been with me since February." Then he called, in a loud voice, "Original-help, come and see your honorable mistress?"

"I am coming, honorable master."

Thus speaking Original-help No. 1 descended from the attic with a lantern in his hand, at the same time Original-help No. 2 entered from the veranda, leading the elder child and carrying the younger in his arms.

In the excitement of beholding his children, Sir Cliff-side forgot the extraordinary phenomenon of the duplicate Original-help, and affectionately rubbing his elder boy on the head, said

"My son, New-six, you have grown quite a big fellow. I am so glad to set eyes upon you again, I hope you have been good and obeyed your mother. I see Help-of-six is afraid of me and hides his head in Original-help's short coat."

New-six looked up anxiously at his father's face and enquired in a gentle voice :

"Dear papa, do your eyes pain you? I am glad I have come, now you will have some one to rub your back, you know that is a good thing to do to sick people?"

Little Help-of-six, encouraged by Original-help No. 2 glanced timidly around and said, "Is my papa sick?" Then, descending from the servant's arms, he toddled toward his parent and fondled him, saying, "I, too, will rub your back, papa. You will soon get quite well."

Sir Cliff-side was moved to tears by the tender

speeches and affectionate manner of his children, and for some moments was unable to speak. At last he held them close to him and said :

" O, both of you have become most gentle. My dear Bamboo, you must feel very tired, lie down without any ceremony and rest."

Bamboo stretched herself upon the mat and the little ones reclined upon their father's knees, while he caressed them and talked with his wife about their dead lord.

Original help No. 2 softly rose and retired to the kitchen where he found Original-help No. 1 busily engaged preparing supper. Although he had heard the man addressed by the same name as himself, he was unaware how exactly they resembled each other.

" Mr. Original-help," he whispered, " I do not wish to disturb our master and mistress who have much to talk about. I have brought from Ako many letters and messages for the attendants on Lady Pure-gem. As it is some distance from here to Blue-hill I wish to start soon. Will you require any aid from me ? "

" No, Mr. Original-help," laughingly answered the other. " You start at once. I will attend to our master and mistress. You need not hurry back to-night. The road between here and Blue-hill is none of the safest. I will explain the reason of your absence to our master."

"Thank you," said Original-help No. 2. "I will return early in the morning."

Sir Cliff-side and his wife had ceased their conversation in order to listen to the foregoing talk, and, when the man departed, the lady said :

" I am very much perplexed by the resemblance between those men. Did you not tell me that your servant was our Original-help ? "

" So he is, Bamboo. He came from Ako in February."

"But, my honorable husband, Original-help has never left me. Your man must be my servant's twin-brother."

" That is impossible," replied Sir Cliff-side. " They are evidently strangers to one another. I am as much puzzled as yourself."

The lady thought for a while, then said in a low, terrified tone :

"My honorable husband, now I understand the mystery. It is a case of the soul-dividing disease."

CHAPTER XVI.

THE GOD FOX.

The ancient book called *Kishitzuho* (prescriptions for strange sicknesses) thus describes the *ri-kon-bio* (soul-dividing disease);

" If any person suddenly becomes two beings, exactly resembling each other, it is a case of soul-dividing disease. You may know this by the fact of the duplicate person being unable to speak. The remedy for such an affliction is as follows :

" Take equal parts of gentian, asafœtida and ginger, pound them in a mortar and make a strong infusion. Give the person who can speak, one *saké* cupful every half hour. The medicine will make the patient bright and cheerful, and cause the duplicate, wandering spirit to return to its proper body.

" This disease is a very rare one."

Sir Cliff-side quoted the fore-going extracts to his wife adding :

" Bamboo, I do not believe any such sickness exists out of books. Doctors are very fond of explaining

things that no human being can fathom. Even, according to their statement, this cannot be a case of
the soul-dividing disease, for both men speak. Do not
permit the affair to worry you. Leave a mystery
alone and it will explain itself. Tell me about Sir
Big-rock and what has brought you hither. See,
our dear children are both fast asleep on my knees.
Leave them so until supper is ready "

Bamboo moved closer to her husband, and, fearing
Original-help No. 1 might be a spy of Kira, whispered

" I have very important news for you. I suppose
you have heard how strangely the chief-councillor has
behaved; how he divorced his wife, gave up the care
of his children and spends his time with the butter-flies
of the tea-houses. Such things would not have been
surprising in an ordinary man, but coming from the
chief-councillor have amazed every one. The conspirators in Kioto have been terribly exercised, spite
of which he carries himself in a most reckless manner
Is this not incomprehensible? Can he have forgotten
the kindnesses of our late lord? "

" Bamboo, I have every faith in Sir Big-rock. We
know of his proceedings, and have many times met
to consult about the matter, finally agreeing to continue our work of watching Kira, and to wait patiently.
Sir Big-rock is not a man to indulge in such pleasures
for the sake of gratifying himself. Our enemy, although skulking in the retirement of his residence,
has immense influence, and is guarded vigilantly. I,

and many of the conspirators, believe Sir Big-rock acts as he does to throw Kira off his guard. If our conjecture is correct all will yet go well, and when the proper moment arrives, Sir Big-rock will give us the signal. Our present anxiety is to learn what are his real sentiments ; Sir Hatchet and Sir Common have this matter in hand, and, being on the spot, know what is best to do. In a few days they will be joined by Sir Thousand-cliffs who will represent the conspirators residing in this city. Now tell me what you have to communicate."

" My honorable master," said Original-help No. 1, speaking from the kitchen, " at last the supper is ready. The honorable wife and master-boys must be very hungry. I am ashamed to say there is nothing good to give them."

The father awoke his children and the servant brought in the repast, which was really a most excellent one and was heartily enjoyed. During the meal Original-help No. 1 laughed with the boys, who in their innocence, took the man to be Original-help No. 2, though the wife was secretly troubled and regarded him askance.

The supper being over, the mother made up beds for her little ones, and, when the attendant had retired for the night, reclined close to her husband and observed in a low tone :

" At last I can speak freely. About a week before I left Ako, the chief-councillor called upon me and

said: ' I am informed Sir Cliff-side has been very
sick and that he has not yet fully recovered. Of course,
under the circumstances, you have desired to be with
him, still, knowing his position, have submitted patiently, fearing lest your presence might interfere with
our plans. That is as it should be and your loyal conduct merits my thanks. I, however, now desire you
will join your husband and take your children with you.
When a man is sick it is not good for him to be left
to the mercy of strangers.' He then gave me thirty
rio for you and ten for my traveling expenses," producing the money. " Honorable husband, although I
have practised the utmost economy, I have only been
able to save four *rio*. The boys were both of them
sick and I had to pay for many extras."

" My dear Bamboo, you have done well to save
anything. This present from the chief-councillor,"
raising the package to his forehead, "gives me double
hope. It shows he has neither forgotten his vow nor
myself."

" Honorable husband, that is not all. The chief-
councillor said : ' Later on I will despatch Sir Hatchet
or Sir Island-in-the-front with money for those who are
in Yedo.' Here," producing another package, " are
thirty-eight *rio* I received for the sale of our house
and furniture, and five *rio* paid me by the District-
overseer. He said : ' I know you must be sorely
pinched by being so suddenly cut off from the income
allowed by your lord, and thinking you needed the

money, have brought five of the ten *rio* I owe your husband.' He expressed the deepest regret at his inability at once to pay the entire sum borrowed of you, and promised to do all in his power soon to liquidate the debt. Though I did not like to act without consulting you, I was so much touched by his goodness, that I gave him a receipt for ten *rio*. Instead of trying to cheat us, like some people I could mention, he did his best."

" I thank you, Bamboo. You acted just as I would have done. The overseer was one of our lord's retainers, yet he lives a great distance from the city, and could safely have assumed a know-nothing face with regard to his debt. I thank the gods there are some honest men in the world."

"Yes, he is honest through and through. At first he refused to take the receipt and, finally, said : ' Tell your honorable husband, after the harvest is over I intend to visit Yedo, when I will call on him and clear my conscience.' Now you have learned what brought me hither, I would like to know about your sickness. How came your eyes in such a state ? "

" Mine is a case of drying up of the water of the pupil. At first, Dr. Original-course felt very anxious about me, saying the only thing to cure my disease would be to use the very best pearls ; yet how could I obtain things of such great value. I believe our lady must have given him some for me as, since February, I have been regularly supplied with them."

"Ah, honorable husband, our lady is very good!"

"Yes, indeed she is. Only to-day she spoke to the doctor about me. So the children were sick during the journey?"

"Yes, at one time I feared little Help-of-six would die. You must know they have both had the small-pox. I was compelled to stay a month in the city of Mulberry and was at my wit's end. Poor Help-of-six, not being as old and sensible as his brother, cried all day, was very irritable, and would never sleep except on my lap. As many as three physicians gave him up, and twice his breathing ceased altogether. But for our good Original-help, I should not be here to-day. He attended upon us with the greatest devotion, going without sleep, treating the boys as his own, and encouraging us by word and deed. I prayed to the gods constantly, and vowed if my children were spared not to eat sugar or oranges for three years, so please don't tempt me with those things. My prayers were heard and the dear boys got well. I have the happiness of presenting them to you without their showing any signs of the trouble. You don't know how much I have endured."

"The gods be praised, they have safely passed through one calamity of their lives. You say Help-of-six suffered the most? That is a thing I cannot understand. New-six, being the elder, should have had most disease in his body, at least so say the doc-tors, though I believe many of their assertions are mere guesses. When I think of the great calamity that has overtaken our lord, I am perfectly willing to die. My duty to him is before all other; still, remembering the uncertain future of our poor babes, I cannot help feeling anxious."

Bamboo wiped her eyes with her sleeves, and gazing earnestly at him, replied :

"My honorable husband, though you cannot leave your children a fortune, you will bequeath them something better—a reputation that will keep them straight through life. All the world is waiting for you and your honorable companions to strike at the cowardly wretch who deprived us of our benevolent and beloved lord. Remember, in the sad days when my eyes will no longer behold you, our two brave boys will constantly visit your tomb, deck it with flowers, and burn incense to your spirit. Let that comfort you."

"My loyal wife, I am ready, at any moment, to do my duty. Your words, indeed, cheer me, for I know after I have gone the Lonely Road, you will bring up our children like true *samurai*."

"Yes, my honorable husband, I will endeavor to do so. You are tired, let me give you your medicine."

She procured the pot, and, while pouring out the liquid, whispered to him :

"I shall not sleep a wink to-night. You are brave and above superstition ; I am only a woman full of the fancies of my sex. I really believe my good Original-help must have had an attack of the soul-dividing disease."

The next morning Original-help No. 2 arrived at the house and found everything ready for breakfast, but Original-help No. 1 was nowhere to be seen.

As Sir Cliff-side, his wife and children, entered the room, the man saluted them and said :

" My honorable master, did your Original-help deliver my respectful message ? "

" No," said Sir Cliff-side, then raising his voice, he shouted : " Original-help, where are you ? "

The echo outside repeated : " Where are you ? "

" Come," said Bamboo to her attendant, " I see you are now all right."

The man hesitated, as though ashamed, and said :

" My honorable mistress, I thought I had walked off all traces of last night's indulgence. The servants of our lady plied me with *saké*. You see they were very glad to get news from Ako and it was first 'drink with me,' then 'drink with me,' until your miserable Original-help was as red as *Shut-ten-do-shi* (the demon of drink). I beg you will forgive me this time."

The lady waited until her husband had gone into the veranda, then whispered to the penitent servant

" Original-help, I am going to tell you something. Do not be alarmed ; you have lately suffered from a dreadful malady."

" Yes, my honorable mistress, *saké* always has

been my weakness. I have a chronic trouble termed dry-throat."

" No, not that, good Original-help. You have been afflicted with a most wonderful complaint, called the soul-dividing disease. One half of you has been here, in Yedo, with my honorable husband, and the other in attendance upon me. Your double has returned to your body. Do not tremble so, you are perfectly cured."

The bewildered man gaped at her, as though fearing she was not in her right senses, but remembering a *samurai* lady must know more than a common fellow like himself, proceeded to dish the breakfast, murmuring as he did so :

" That fellow, who called himself Original-help, like me ? If I thought I looked as homely as he does, I would go and drown myself."

In a little while he announced the meal was ready, and the family seated themselves. They had scarcely begun to eat when a paper fluttered in through the porch and fell at Sir Cliff-side's feet.

" What is this ? " he cried, picking it up, then read its contents, which were as follows :

" Since last February I have assumed the form and manner of your servant, Original-help, and nursed you during your sickness. Now your family and attendant have arrived from Ako, you no longer require my aid. Your eyes are fast getting well, yet be advised by me and continue taking the pearls. I have left a good number of them for you in the hands of your doctor, who believes they came from Lady Pure-gem. Using my supernatural power I assumed the shape of a merchant, and—while punishing that avaricious quack, Dr. Butterfly-cottage, who, forgetting the benefits conferred upon him by his former lord, is consorting with your enemies—obtained what you so sadly needed. You may expect still further assistance from me.

"To Sir Cliff-side ;

"From an inhabitant of the residence of Lady Pure-gem."

After reading this the *samurai* remarked to his amazed wife and servant

"Then the one whom I deemed to be a man was the god Fox of the residence of our lady. He has taken pity upon me and saved me much suffering. How can I forget his great mercy!"

Overcome by this discovery the three shed tears of gratitude ; while the children, witnessing their emotion, uttered piercing cries and wept as profusely as their elders.

When Sir Cliff-side recovered the full use of his sight, he paid a visit to Lady Pure-gem, to whom he related the wonderful story here recorded. She was greatly moved by the miraculous interposition of the god, and, assembling her attendants, reverently made offerings at his shrine.

From that time he was referred to as the "Omnipo-
tent god Fox Original-help," which name he contin-
ues to bear to the present day.

If the reader desires to satisfy himself of this fact, he
has only to visit the Blue-hill district where he will
find the shrine, which is kept in beautiful order by the
neighboring inhabitants ; yet there are some sceptics
who sneer at the supernatural powers of the god Fox.

CHAPTER XVII.

CONVOLVULUS OVERHEARS A CONVERSATION.

"The cherry blossoms were blusing in the temple gardens ; the air was mild and full of vernal incense sent up to the flowers to the gods ; the swiftly-flowing water of the Kamo River glittered like the spears of a vast army ; pic-nic parties swarmed out to the hills surrounding the city ; and all creation revelled in the warm sunshine."

On such a day as this, Sir Big-rock was seen staggering along Temple Street, Kioto. He was dressed in a black costume, marked with his crest, and carried himself with the exaggerated dignity of a man who has taken an extra cup ; seeing which the beggars and tradesmen nimbly got out of his way, knowing, from experience, that the sword of a drunken *samurai* rests uneasily in its scabbard. As he turned the corner of Temple Avenue he was stopped by a *ronin* wearing a pilgrim's hat, who saluted him, and said in a low tone :

" Well met, Sir Big-rock, I have been looking for you everywhere."

The councillor steadied himself against the trunk of a cherry-tree, and, peering at the speaker through his half-closed eye-lids, replied :

" Well met, Sir Common. I was just hoping to see some thirsty friend who would assist me in emptying a bottle of the best. There is an excellent shop not far from here, where the *Bozu* (Buddhist priests) obtain their nourishment. Come along, come along."

Thus speaking, he grasped Sir Common by the arm and led him down a side-street to an inn called the " Eight Supreme Delights." When they were seated in a private room, Sir Common began to question his friend with regard to his intentions concerning Sir Kira. Sir Big-rock listened indifferently, and presently remarked

" We came to drink, not talk about impossible things. It is useless for a sickle-insect to attack a team of horses. Is that all you have to tell me ? "

Sir Common lowered his voice to a whisper and said :

" Honorable comrade, I have something important to communicate. Do you remember the woman who was lately attendant upon your children ? She called herself Peach-blossom."

" Yes, I recollect the creature ; her true name was Convolvulus. She was a spy of Sir Kira and is the wife of Black-field, his trusted retainer. I, at one time, thought of using her as a means of deceiving her mas-ter, but now have given up the idea. She lives not far from here, next door to a very worthy man who is a money-changer. I spent last evening at his house, and he was so hospitable that on my way home I dropped one of my swords. When you met me I was endeavoring to find it."

"I understand, honorable comrade, Convolvulus listens to everything that passes between you and your friend. Her husband and a band of Kira's people are secreted in her house, waiting for a chance to kill you. They have been following you for several months. Be warned by me, and do not go near the place to-night."

As he ceased speaking he looked at Sir Big-rock, whom, to his annoyance, he found fast asleep; noticing which he arose and summoning the landlord, said :

"This noble *samurai* is suffering from over-fatigue. Here is a *rio*, I pray you let him remain as long as he desires. When he awakens, give him some of your best *saké*, and do everything in your power to detain him here all night. I will call again to-morrow."

He quitted the room, and the landlord, closing the door after him, significantly replied :

"Judging by your honorable friend's symptoms, he will not awaken until sunset. Your instructions shall be strictly followed."

No sooner had Sir Common departed than Sir Big-rock arose, and reassuming an intoxicated expression, staggered out of the apartment and, spite of the land-

lord's persuasion, sallied into the street.   His zig-zag
walk highly amused a number of children, who, falling
into line, mimicked his gestures and followed him as
far as the house of the money-changer.

Sir Big-rock seated himself upon the edge of the
platform at the entrance to the store, which was shaded
by an over-hanging pine tree, and glanced drowsily at
the proprietor, who, after saluting him respectfully,
ordered his boy to bring some tea, then observed :

" Honorable sir, I presume you have come for your
sword ? " producing the weapon and handing it to his
visitor.   " My boy found it lying on the *tokonoma* in
the back room."

At that moment the lad came forward with the cup
of tea on a small lacquered tray and kneeling near the
guest, presented it, thinking as he did so :

" The honorable *samurai* is very much confused this
morning   what comical grimaces he makes."

Sir Big-rock did not take the cup, being busily engaged in attempting to draw the sword from its sheath.
While he was thus employed Mrs. Convolvulus
emerged from a neighboring house, and noiselessly approaching the money-changer's residence, listened at a
side window.

" This sword," said Sir Big-rock, " was presented to
me by my late lord.   There are people who reproach
me for not having avenged his death.   I laugh at all
such idiots.   What can one person do against a powerful noble like Sir Kira.   Moreover, remembering

Sir Big-rock did not take the cup, being busily engaged in attempting to draw the sword from its sheath.

Chap. xvii, p. 216.

the saying, ' man's life is but fifty years,' who would care to shorten it. Turning to the boy he murmured " *Saké*? Yes, I can always take a cup."

" This is Uzi tea," responded the lad, stifling an inclination to snicker.

" The honorable *samurai* knows that," said the money-changer, frowning at his servant. " Why did you not bring *saké* as I directed ? "

The boy retired and on reaching the rear apartment, performed a pantomimic dance, and sang to himself:

" *Saké* and tea are all the same to a man who has been to see the flowers."

" Mr. Gold-help," hiccoughed the visitor, as though replying to an invitation, " certainly, certainly, I will visit you again this evening."

" You honor me, Sir Big-rock. At what time may I expect you ?"

" About the hour of the Hog (8 P. M.)," drowsily answered his guest. " We will indulge in a royal carouse."

" You shall have some more of that old *saké*," said the delighted merchant.

" Good, good ! " muttered the other " I cannot wait now. Permit me to leave this sword here until tonight. It will never do for me to go through the streets at mid-day with three weapons in my girdle. People might imagine me to be intoxicated."

As he rose to depart he saw the shadow of Convolvulus vanish from the window.

About the hour of the Rat (midnight), when most honest men were slumbering, Sir Big-rock quitted the house of the money-changer. The latter had long been oblivious of anything his guest said, and was lying on his back, with his right arm in a dish of stewed lampreys. His visitor had done the talking and he the drinking; though the tradesman imagined the reverse.

The *samurai* assumed an intoxicated air and walked very eccentrically, pausing frequently to gaze at the moon. He did not appear to observe three men who had emerged from a neighboring tenement and, sword in hand, were creeping after him, their bare feet making no sound upon the pavement. After going some distance he turned down a lane and entered a lonely spot at the rear of the shrine of Hachiman (the god of war). In the midst of the ground was a gnarled, feathery pine, the trunk of which was completely shaded by the drooping branches. Sir Big-rock staggered toward the tree and placed his back against the stem, when, all of a sudden, the men rushed forward and attempted to cut him down.

This proved a very difficult task, he being in the shadow and his assailants in the full light of the moon; added to which he fought with the greatest coolness and skill. The bravos finding they were getting the worst of it, took to their heels, never stopping until they reached the house of Convolvulus, who expended a large package of paper in patching their mutilated bodies.

They forgot to report the result of their encounter to Kira, and as their intended victim kept his own counsel, the loyal ronins remained in ignorance of the affair.

From that time the spies contented themselves with watching Sir Big-rock and reporting his vagaries to their master, who, as the days passed, gradually began to regard his enemy with profound contempt.

CHAPTER XVIII.·

SIR UNCONQUERABLE PERFORMS AN ACT OF JUSTICE.

" An arrow aimed at a private soldier sometimes slays a general.
A chance word is often more effective than a premeditated
speech."

In the vicinity of Kamakura, within bowshot of
the great bronze image of Buddha, was a fashionable inn, that, in the spring of 1701, was conducted by
two men and a woman, whose dialect betrayed them
to be natives of Ako, though they assured every one
they had come from the South.

Their establishment was managed in a very peculiar way, none of the servants being permitted to remain in the house at night, and strange rumors were
circulated regarding the proprietors, who were said to
be bandits.   One of them was an old man called
Quick-sand, and the other, who was supposed to be his
relative, was addressed as Long-radish ; though few
imagined those were their true names.   Both stood in
the greatest fear of the hostess, who, while she sat in her

private room and enjoyed every luxury, ordered them about like beggars, and compelled them to do the work of four servants. This woman had a very hot tongue, and ruled the house, even the guests sometimes experiencing the effect of her temper.

One evening Sir Unconquerable, dressed as of old and wearing his *ronin* hat, presented himself at the inn, and marching into the best apartment, ordered refreshments, at the same time curtly announcing that he intended to remain all night.

A few days before, he had been told of the bad reputation borne by the establishment, on hearing which he felt a burning desire to visit it ; his old spirit of adventure prompting him to go where hard knocks were likely to be given and taken. He was also informed Sir Kira's chief-councillor was in the habit of frequenting the inn.

When the attendant had delivered the new-comer's order to her mistress, she said :

" I do not keep a house for the entertainment of poor *samurai*."

" Mrs. Rose-bud; he is not poor. I believe he is Sir Plain-field who made a large sum of money by the misfortunes of his lord. He carries a big purse."

" Big purse, does he ? That settles the case. You are not beautiful enough to wait on such a valuable guest ; send Tiger-lily here. She is the one to make him order expensive food and drink."

While the grim-visaged *ronin* was being served,

her husband and his partner entered her room, when she said :

" Quick-sand and Long-radish, go and look through the spy-hole at our new guest. He is laden with money. You will have to attend to him to-night."

The elder of the men put on his horn-spectacles, and advancing to a place where some holes had been made in the wall, peeped,—then began to tremble.

" Are you going to have a stroke ? " she snapped. " What has overtaken you ? "

He turned his ashen features toward her and hoarsely whispered :

" Ye gods ! it is Sir Unconquerable ! Now the end has arrived and we shall have to give up what we have stolen."

" Phewgh ! " she returned. " We will do no such thing. You were always a coward, Arrow-stand. Who cares for Sir Unconquerable ? "

" But, honorable madame," faltered the other man, " Unconquerable is a perfect demon. Our lives are not worth a cash each."

" Listen," she said. " He does not know my face, I will go and entertain him. To-night, when he is happily sleeping, you can rid us of his troublesome presence."

" Steal his swords, my dear," suggested her husband, in a tremulous voice. " We dare not attack him while he is armed."

"Leave it all to me," she said. "You become more timorous every day. Cease quaking and look like a man. That old *saké* will conquer him!"

At the hour of the rat (mid-night) Sir Unconquerable saw the door of his room pushed back, and by the dim light from the corridor, beheld two men enter the apartment. In an instant he was upon his feet, and as the intruders attacked him with their long swords, seized one by the neck and the other by the sleeve and hurled them to the floor, then picking up a weapon, dropped by the elder of the two, proceeded to demonstrate the strength of his arm. The intruders uttered loud cries, on hearing which the landlady, spear in hand, rushed upon the scene and assisted in entertaining their guest.

Alas for their calculations! In a short time the thread of her existence was severed, and her husband and his partner were extended on the mats in the agonies of death.

The tumult had aroused the other guests, who crowded into the chamber and demanded the cause of the disturbance. Sir Unconquerable explained what had occurred, and calling for a light, observed :

"Let us take a look at these rascally inn-keepers."

A lamp being brought he discovered who they were, whereupon he sternly exclaimed :

"So, it is you, unfaithful, disloyal wretches. While striking in the dark I have accomplished an act of justice. The vengeance of heaven may be slow but it is sure. Now I shall sleep comfortably."

Thus perished those contemptible creatures, Sir Arrow-stand and Sir Wisteria-lake, whose lives, like their deaths, were miserable.

CHAPTER XIX.

MISS QUIET'S DOWER.

In chapter the sixth I described how three *ronin-samurai* presented themselves at the castle of Ako and offered their services to avenge the death of Lord Morning-field. Although Sir Big-rock could not then avail himself of their aid, he determined to communicate with them later on, as he knew they were men whose loyalty was beyond question. A few days after the surrender of the castle, one of the three, Sir Cliff-field was seized with a fatal sickness which confined him to his bed. On finding his end near he sent for his son, a youth of sixteen, to whom he was tenderly attached. When the boy had saluted him, he grasped his short sword in his right hand and said

" My son, I am about to climb the Hill of Death and shall soon arrive at the place where the three roads meet. I do not desire to take the one leading to the infernal regions, or the path from this world, preferring, as I am a good Buddhist, to go to *Gokuraku* (Paradise). When *Sanzu-no-baba* (the old woman who is the toll-keeper of the Sanzu-river) comes forward to receive my clothes, she will ask me why I bring this sword with me. I have therefore determined to give it to you."

He paused, through weakness, and his daughter said: " My honorable father, let me give you a cup of tea, it will cheer your spirits."

The dying man waited until she had served him, then bade her retire and said to his son :

" This morning I was reading the book you see before me. It is the history of *Kusunoki Masashige*, which you, of course, know by heart. I desire to follow the example of that mirror of loyalty and bequeath a legacy to you. Soon after the surrender of the castle of Ako, Sir Big-rock privately sent for me, and to my delight admitted me into the noble band of men who have vowed to avenge the death of our never-to-be-forgotten chief. The gods have decreed that the thread of my life shall soon be snapped. I charge you to take this sword, the gift of our dead chief, and to assume the responsibility of my vow, so that my spirit may pass happily to a future state."

He slowly recited the oath he had taken, his boy repeating the words after him and receiving the sword, which he solemnly swore to use as his father directed.

" Farewell, my son," exclaimed the old *ronin*. " When I meet our lord in Paradise, I shall not be ashamed to look upon his face."

The young Sir Cliff-field buried his father, and after mourning sixty days, went to Sir Big-rock, who was much moved by the loyal devotion of the *samurai*, and accepted him as a member of the conspiracy. He was directed to assume the name of Three-help, and ordered to Yedo, where he joined Sir Cyprus-village, who had opened a grocery called the Three Springs, on a street not far from the residence of Sir Kira.

Sir Cliff-field entered into business with the greatest ardor, and being very handsome, attracted many customers to the shop. Among these were the servants of Sir Kira, whom he treated with special civility, hoping thereby to gain admittance to the noble's mansion. In this he was doomed to disappointment, for, though he gave many bribes, he was never so much as invited into the porter's lodge.

One day a young girl named Miss Quiet, a nurse-maid in the service of Sir Small-grove, entered the Three Springs, and asked for a cake of *tofu* (bean-curd). Sir Cliff-field, who received her order, said in an insinuating tone :

" It is a shame you should be obliged to carry this home. Will you permit me to take it for you ? "

" You are too kind," she replied, modestly closing her eyes. " I am only a poor little servant girl."

" You are very beautiful," he whispered. " Do you not reside in the honorable house of Sir Kira ? "

She answered in the affirmative, and finally accepted

his offer. From that day Miss Quiet ·became a constant visitor at the store.

Some of the shop-men, who were not in the conspiracy, wondered how a good-looking fellow like Three-help could fall in love with such a homely girl as Miss Quiet, and passed many witty remarks upon the matter, to all of which he would reply

"The sensible man looks to the heart. The morning-glory soon withers."

In the course of a few months Miss Quiet accepted the young grocer as her betrothed and introduced him to her uncle, Mr. Plain, a retired architect, who lived snugly upon the earnings of his younger days, in a comfortable house on Divinity Street.

The girl loved her affianced very tenderly, yet never invited him to visit her at her master's residence, which, being within the enclosure containing Sir Kira's mansion, was guarded closely. The meetings of the lovers always took place at her uncle's home, and the young people did not appear together upon the street.

After awhile Sir Cliff-field became really enamored with her; notwithstanding which he eagerly kept his eyes and ears open, and was as anxious as ever to gain admission to Sir Kira's mansion.

Who can predict what sort of chicken will be hatched from an egg.

This *samurai* who had, in the beginning, made certain plans, found them defeated by his attachment to

" Three-help, you will have great pleasure in looking at these beautiful drawings."

this humble but virtuous girl; still, in the end, it was through her he obtained what he so greatly desired.

At first the old architect treated him very coolly, but when he found the young people really loved each other, he gradually took a liking to the grocer and called him nephew, while Sir Cliff-field, who highly esteemed the old man, addressed him by the familiar title of uncle.

One day, in July, 1701, when the lovers were paying the architect a visit, he produced a number of plans, which he proudly exhibited, saying:

" Let me show you some of my handiwork."

" Excuse me, honorable uncle, I must go," said his niece, rising and stepping into the "mouth of the house" where she slipped on her clogs. " *Sayonara* (farewell). Three-help, you will have great pleasure in looking at those beautiful drawings. You must not accompany me, for, if I were seen walking with any one, my mistress would dismiss me from her service. In our house we have to be doubly particular. That fidgety old Sir Kira suspects everybody."

As soon as she had departed, the architect said :

" What do you think of these specimens ?"

" You have wonderful talent, uncle. This must be a plan of a *daimio's* mansion. Have you designed many such ? "

" Yes, a great number. I drew the plan of Sir Kira's *yashiki* (mansion). He was very crotchety and gave me lots of trouble. This," unrolling a large paper, " is what I did for him. It contains more passages and secret rooms than a fashionable tea-house."

" What a beautiful piece of work. How I envy you the ability to do such a thing."

" That is nothing, nephew. I really ought not to keep this, yet on account of its exquisite finish, hesitate to destroy it. When I die you must be very careful with my papers ; I am like a doctor, I know the mysteries of many houses."

He rolled up the drawings and showed the young man a recess beneath the *tokonoma* where he kept his treasures, as he did so, remarking :

" You, without doubt, remember how the Lord of Ako was treated by Sir Kira, do you not, nephew ? "

" Yes, uncle, I know something about the matter ; will you kindly give me the full particulars ? "

The old man related the story of the tragedy and concluded his narration by saying :

" Although I once had Sir Kira for a client I heartily detest him. The Lord of Ako was a noble man, just and humane. I am amazed that his retainers have not avenged his death. I know it is wrong to talk in this manner, still, were I a *samurai*, I would never rest until I had done my duty."

" Uncle, you forget the law forbids men taking justice into their own hands. No doubt the members of the clan have loyal hearts—they do not desire to oppose the authorities."

This reply made the architect very angry.

"Go to," he cried. "Were you a *samurai*, you would not utter such words."

"I am a *samurai*," was the proud response. "My true name is Cliff-field."

The architect leaned back upon his elbows, and regarding his visitor with amazement, joyfully exclaimed :

"Well met, Sir Cliff-field, I am Green-mountain, who was once a councillor of the Lord of Tamba, the bosom friend of Lord Morning-field. Through the intrigues of a fellow-official, I lost the favor of my honored chief and was forced to become a *ronin*. Though I wear the garb of a tradesman I have the heart of a *samurai*. I believe I understand what you are doing in Yedo." Taking the plans from their hiding place, he continued : "Future nephew, here are some important papers, accept them as the dower of my niece."

Sir Cliff-field received the documents with trembling hands, and raising them to his forehead, murmured :

"Sir Green-mountain, future uncle, I cannot find words with which to express my thanks. You give your niece a priceless dower. Up to this time the hearts of my loyal comrades have been sorely troubled, and we have hoped against hope. Our enemy, strong in his political power, guarded like the Sho-gun himself, has defied our attempts and mocked at our misery. Your kindness will enable us to clear the stain of disloyalty from the name of the clan of Ako."

Within ten days the plan was delivered into the hands of Sir Big-rock, who, after examining it, exclaimed :

" I see one star shining through the darkness of the night."

CHAPTER XX.

Even a high mountain may in time become a hillock.
How a few vows stand the test of years."

Upon a hot day in August, 1701, Sir Big-rock was
seated in his library, thinking of the news he had
received from Yedo.

"Only one thing is now required," he said,
thinking aloud. "Kira has sent away the guard
furnished by his son, and evidently no longer fears
me. I will now try the loyalty of the conspirators,
and when I have winnowed the rice, proceed to Yedo
and carry out the plan I have so long had in my
mind. It is most certain Kira will never give us an
opportunity to attack him upon the street, so we will
storm his residence and kill the badger in his hole.
Had I not obtained the plan from Sir Cliff-field we
should have been compelled to grope our way in the
dark ; I now know every nook and corner of our
enemy's house better than he does.".

" You must excuse us to-day. Pardon me, Sir Big-rock, why are we thus mistrusted? What are we to understand by your words? Surely you do not intend that Sir Kira shall die in his bed. Are the sacrifices and sufferings of the loyal clansmen, of our wives, children and dependants to go for nothing, like bubbles that rise on the surface of water. This long delay has sorely tried many of our number, and we fear some of them may lose heart, and when the time comes, refuse to perform their vow. You must surely comprehend all these things. We have come to ask you, once and for all, what is your determination with regard to our enemy."

" Yes, Chief-councillor," said Sir Hatchet, " Sir Common has exactly expressed my sentiments. Many of the conspirators, discouraged by this long delay, are losing their grip."

" I understand," calmly answered Sir Big-rock. " In the beginning, carried away by anger and a desire for revenge, I made up my mind, come what might, to attack Sir Kira. I now think better of it. All the reports show any attempt on our part would result in ignominious defeat. I do not desire to become the laughing-stock of the world, and thus bring additional disgrace upon the memory of our honored lord. Our best plan will be again to petition the Council of Elders to reëstablish the house of Ako. That is my idea; what do you think? "

Sir Common, who had listened most impatiently, angrily replied :

"I do not agree with you! I never expected to hear such words from the mouth of Sir Big-rock. You know full well the council has not the slightest intention to grant what you propose. We have waited nearly three years for them to move in the matter, and might wait three hundred, could we live so long. There is only one course open to us, namely, to take the head of Sir Kira, and thus wipe out our too prolonged disgrace."

"You jump at conclusions," said Sir Big-rock. "The fact of our having conspired has reached the ears of the authorities at Yedo, who naturally agree that, as long as we entertain such feelings, we are unworthy to be restored to our old positions. I have thought the matter over and have resolved to return the written oaths intrusted to my charge. It would be making the affair too important were I specially to summon the late conspirators for that purpose. I will therefore give the papers into your charge. When you come across our friends, communicate my ideas to them, and return their pledges."

He then took a roll of documents from his writing-desk and held the package toward them.

For some moments the visitors remained speechless with indignation.

"Sir Big-rock," cried Sir Common, "are you endeavoring to fathom our hearts? I did not take that oath in jest. If you mean what you say, Chief-councillor as you are, I will not spare you."

Having thus spoken he grasped the hilt of his sword and impatiently waited for a reply.

" Sir Common, you provoke yourself about a trifle. If my decision does not suit you and others, follow your own judgment, only exclude me from your arrangements, as I have a plan of my own. All I ask you is to take charge of these papers."

" I will not accept them," thundered Sir Common. " Have you forgotten the sacred charge I brought from Yedo? Go to the temple of the Snow-clad Pine and refresh your loyalty by gazing at the last gift from your lord. If, after that, you refuse to keep your vow, I will cut off your head and offer it to the god of war, which act will show our fellow conspirators that, at least, they have one man who is not afraid to lead them! These are strong words to use to a Chiefcouncillor, but this is no time for compliments. My heart is full of sorrow for my dead lord, therefore my tongue brooks not the restraint of ceremony. I will call upon you to-morrow, in order to receive your reply."

Sir Hatchet waited a few moments, then interposed, saying :

" Calm yourself, Sir Common. I begin to understand the meaning of Sir Big-rock's words. We will do as he desires and receive the documents."

" What ? " cried Sir Common, trembling with rage. " Are you, too, a coward ?"

" Come," said Sir Hatchet, grasping his companion

by the arm and hurriedly saluting their leader. " I will take charge of the papers. The Chief-councillor has determined wisely. We will retire."

The next day, while Sir Hatchet was perusing a volume of ancient poems, his daughter came to him and said :

" Honorable father, there is a fan-dealer outside."

" Thank you, Plum. I do not require any of his wares this morning."

The girl retired, but presently returned with a folded paper which she handed to her parent, who, upon opening it, said :

" My dear Plum, will you please send the gentleman in ? "

When the stranger entered, Sir Hatchet saluted him, and exclaimed :

" Welcome, Sir Thousand-cliffs, you have arrived at a most opportune time."

" Dear me," cried the young lady, who was lingering at the door. " Honorable sir, can it be possible you are my cousin, Thousand-cliffs ? I did not know you. How completely you are disguised."

The *samurai*, who was dressed in the humble garb of a merchant, deposited his sample box upon the floor, and wiping his perspiring brow, turned to the lady and replied :

" So you did not recognize me, cousin Plum ? Don't you think I make a good-looking fan merchant ? "

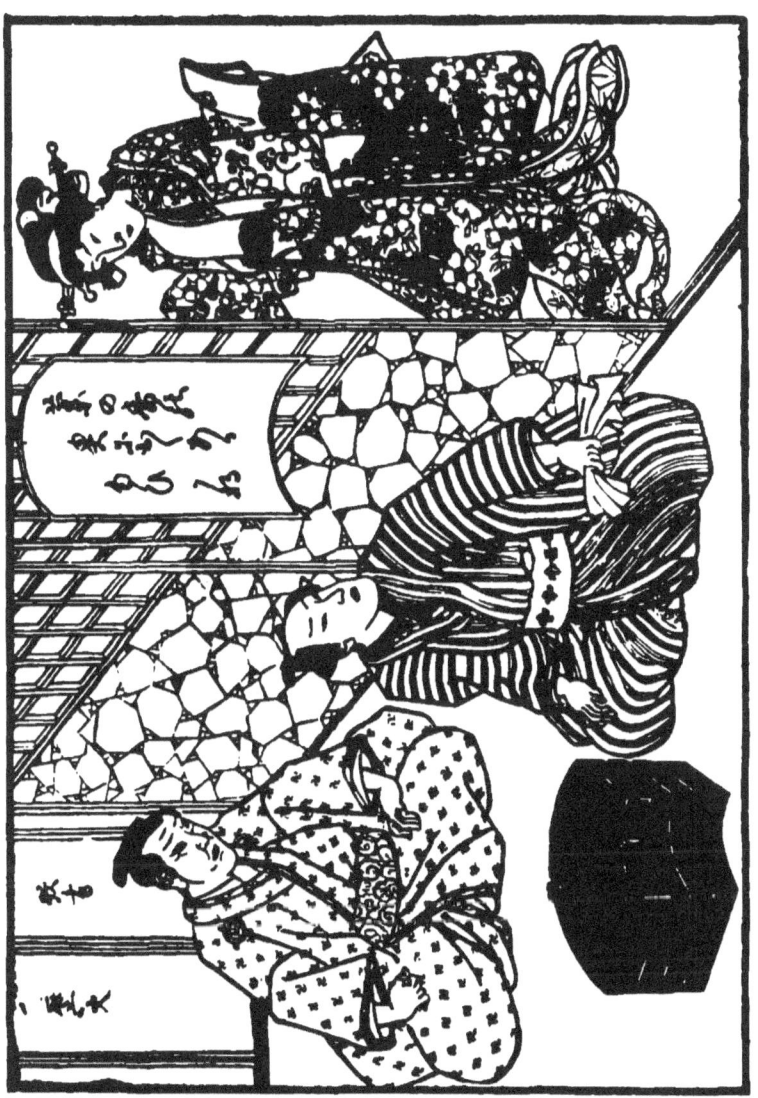

"So you did not recognize me, cousin Plum? Don't you think I make a good-looking fan-merchant?"

Chap. xɪ, p. ɪ48.

we shall act as one person. They, like refined gold,
have been thrice tried. Never mind what may be the
odds we will accomplish our purpose. Do not doubt
me, I am for the attack. Now you know what is in
my heart. I would, however, caution you about one
thing ; be more vigilant than ever. You remember
the saying of Iyeyasu, ' After a victory knot the cords
of your helmet.' "

He then showed his visitors the plan of Sir Kira's
residence, and consulted with them.

Sir Hatchet and Sir Common were so encouraged
and pleased, that they felt as though they were climb-
ing up to heaven.

CHAPTER XXI.

"The samurai lady has the soul of a warrior.
When the son hesitates, the mother leads."

Sir Big-rock having returned the written oaths and ascertained the intentions of his followers, felt in a position to execute his plans. Knowing the clansmen in Yedo were beginning to exhibit impatience, and fearing they might precipitate matters by ill-timed action, he determined to send a representative to pacify and watch over them, for which purpose he summoned Sir Common, whom he thus addressed :

"I have been considering the intelligence brought from Yedo by Sir Thousand-clifis, and would much like to visit our comrades, however, at present that is impossible ; besides my appearance among them would re-awaken Sir Kira's suspicions and defeat our project. I, therefore, desire you will take my place. When can you be ready to depart ? "

Sir Common bowed and replied :

" I offer you my heartfelt thanks for selecting me, a

man of inferior judgment and little wisdom, to represent you on this important mission. Nothing would give me greater pleasure than to start at once, but I have one favor to ask. My aged mother, my wife and child are at my home in Middle Village, near Ako. If I go to Yedo now, I cannot expect to return. For this reason I am most anxious to once more see my dear mother and family, and to bid them a last farewell. Although I cannot openly speak the words, I can, at least, do so mentally. Will it be possible for you to grant me this great indulgence? I shall only be absent one or two days."

Sir Big-rock nodded and answered :

" Everybody thinks of his mother, especially you who have always been such a dutiful and affectionate son. I will grant your request with the greatest pleasure. By all means visit your home and do not be stingy with your farewells. A few days' delay will be of trifling consequence, as Sir Thousand-cliffs will have somewhat quieted the apprehensions of our brothers in Yedo. Present my regards to your honorable mother and family. The perfume of the plum-blossom soon passes away. Make the most of the delightful moments."

The tears stood in the eyes of Sir Common as he respectfully took his leave. He felt that Sir Big-rock was allowing him a happiness he denied himself.

Sir Common purchased a few presents, which he made into a bundle to be carried over his shoulders, then dressed himself in his best, and putting on his striped cloth overcoat, proceeded upon his way, the journey occupying one day and a half. On nearing home his thoughts reverted to the time of his prosperity, when he was a great *samurai* with an allowance of three hundred *koku* of rice.

" Ah ! " he exclaimed, " then I was enabled to lodge my mother in a beautiful residence, now all I can afford is yonder mean cottage. My breast is well nigh closed." (An expression of suppressed grief.)

He paused, and regarding the humble abode, the white roof of which could be seen peeping from among the branches of the pine-trees, dashed the tears from his eyes, and restraining his emotion, assumed an unconcerned air, murmuring to himself :

" It will not do for my mother to see me looking miserable."

As he approached the dwelling he heard his wife, Mrs. Cloth, singing, and knew by the sound of splashing water that she was washing linen. He noiselessly advanced from behind the reed-fence, and halting, watched her, she being unaware of his presence.

Mrs. Cloth, who had her babe upon her back and her sleeves bound with her *tasuke* (a cord carried by ladies to loop up their dresses), was seated upon a clog behind a shallow tub. As she vigorously rubbed the garment and plunged it into the water, she talked to her child, never for a moment imagining he was fast asleep and that his father was listening to what she said.

" Yes, my brave son," she exclaimed, " have a little patience ; eat heartily and enjoy yourself, so that when your papa returns he will not recognize his big, strong Fusa Bo " (literally Apartment baby).

Mrs. Cloth then sang a nursery song, and not hearing his voice in reply ; turned to look at him, when she beheld Sir Common, whereupon she ceased her occupation and said :

" Oh, honorable husband, I am so glad to see you! Mother has been feeling very anxious on your account. Honorable mother, where are you ? My husband has come home ! "

Hearing this, Sir Common's mother, who was over eighty years old, advanced to the window in the side of the entry, and gazing lovingly at her son, said :

" Common, I am delighted once more to behold your face. You must have suffered greatly during this season of returning heat (Indian summer). I pray you not to trouble yourself about saluting me. Lave your feet and enter without ceremony."

" As you please, honorable mother," was his respectful answer. " Your happiness at seeing me is not greater than mine at beholding you."

He slipped off his straw sandals, and laying aside his sun-hat, entered the house, his wife following with the child.

Having prostrated himself and performed the respectful salutation, Sir Common said :

" Honorable mother, I have for a long time expected

"Oh, honorable husband, I am so glad to see you! Mother has been very anxious on your account."

Chap. xii, p. 154.

to come back, in order to ascertain the good or bad
that has occurred to you, but the pressure of business
has detained me."

The aged lady smiled kindly upon him and replied :

" I understand, my son.   Although you were unable
to visit me you have written very frequently from Kioto.
This has afforded me great comfort.   I have not seen
you for six months, yet cannot observe any change in
your appearance.   Your presence fills my heart with
happiness.   During your absence our good Cloth has
been most affectionate, and has proved an admirable
daughter.   Look at our darling Fusa Bo.   Has he not
grown ?   He is very healthy, and can almost balance
himself upon his feet.   He also says a few words, and
is most lovable.   See the pretty fellow ; he is still
asleep, little thinking his papa has come home."

When she ceased speaking, Sir Common's wife took
up the current of the old lady's thought, and said :

" We knew you would feel proud of our boy   A
moment before you came he was talking to me, not in
words that every one could understand, but in his own
baby language.   In an instant, he was off to the dream-
country and I felt his soft cheek rest upon my neck.
Since our honorable mother loves and pets him so
much, he is always about her, and, during the day, she
is his nurse and guardian."

" He is truly a fortunate fellow," said the delighted
father.   " I pray you not to disturb him.   When he

awakens we will make each other's acquaintance. Tell
me where my brother, Total-three, is ? "

" He has only gone to a neighbor's," said Mrs. Cloth,
then, listening for a moment, added : " Here he comes."

As she spoke his brother entered, and saluted Sir
Common with respectful delight.

While the *samurai* were conversing, Mrs. Cloth,
assisted by the old lady, who disliked to be unoccu-
pied, cooked fish and rice and warmed *saké*. When
the baby awoke, the family sat down to a feast and
celebrated the safe return of its head, their happiness
being unmixed and unrestrained.

Sir Common waited until the smiling face of his
parent indicated a good opportunity for him to communicate what he desired to say, then observed :

" My honorable mother, since I have been away
from you in Kioto, I have done my best to find some
place where I could settle and repair my fortune.
Luckily I have met a certain prince of the Kuwan
To provinces, who desires me to enter his service, so
I am about to go to Yedo. I have come hither to announce this happy news and bid you farewell ; I must
start to-morrow morning, but will return next spring
and take you to my new home. Until that time I beg
you will regard my brother, Total-three, as the head
of the family, and remain well and happy. Brother and
wife, you now know my errand. Take every care of
our honored mother. This," producing a sum of
money, " will serve for your present needs. Remember
our honorable mother must not suffer for anything."

Total-three received the package and, like Cloth, felt sad at the thought of losing Sir Common almost as soon as they had recovered him.

" My honorable brother," said the young man, " rest assured nothing shall be lacking on my part."

" Nor on mine," murmured Mrs. Cloth.

While they were speaking, the venerable lady watched the face of her eldest born, and, correcting her attitude (assuming a serious pose), observed

" My son, I am very happy to hear you are going to Yedo, though I would, if possible, like to know the real reason of your journey."

" What does my honored mother mean ? " he cried, affecting amazement. " Have I not fully stated my business ? "

" My son," she gravely replied, " there is no one here but our family and you can speak without restraint. I presume your telling us a certain prince is to take you into his service is a fiction, and am sure the real reason for your trip to Yedo is to avenge the death of our lord. Do you fear to tell me the truth, believing that I, one in ten thousand, might prevent you from going, or that my tears would weaken the vow you have made ? I comprehend your motive for concealment, but you misunderstand me. Woman as I am, the proud mother of *samurai*, I will not give way to undisciplined feeling. I conjure you to speak out, so that there will be no after regret concerning the matter."

Sir Common, surprised and delighted that his mother's loyalty was as true as the needle to the pole, was about to reveal all, when he checked himself, imagining, though she spoke so bravely, when the time came for her to say farewell she would become distracted with grief. This determined him to continue his loving deception. Placing both hands upon the floor, he respectfully said :

" Honorable mother, I grieve to hear your suspicions, as I deemed my explanation would be satisfactory. With regard to avenging the death of our honored lord, the matter is still undecided. While we held the castle we had many consultations, and were resolved to kill Sir Kira. Since that time a great number of our comrades have changed their minds, and even Sir Big-rock is trying to mend his fortune by entering into business. Why should I deceive my honored mother ? I pray you to banish your suspicions and wait until spring, when I will return from Yedo."

While his tongue uttered these words, his heart rebelled against the deceit he was practising upon his parent, and he bowed his head close to the mat, in order to hide his shame.

His mother understood his feelings, but pretending not to do so, answered :

" Since you say so, I am re-assured, and will anxiously wait for the spring to come. My dear son, I pray you be careful of yourself upon your journey.

Start at sunrise, do not travel during the heated hours of noon, and avoid the evening dews. You must be tired. Have a good rest to-night. I will awaken you early."

He thanked her for her minute and careful concern, and after saying good night, retired to rest.

The next morning the old lady arose before daybreak and busied herself in preparing luncheon for him, making rice cakes and other delicacies of which she knew he was very fond.

When Sir Common came from his apartment and beheld her thus employed, he endeavored to appear cheerful, while she thought to herself

" Whatever others may do, it shall not be said that his mother, by word or deed, caused him to be untrue to his lord."

After the morning meal had been eaten, he took his little child upon his knee, and, gazing lovingly at him, said in a low, tender voice :

" My son, your father is going upon a long journey. You must be a very good boy. I shall often think of you and of the comfort you will be to your grandmother and mother. Grow strong, my second self, grow strong. Farewell—my boy ! "

Thus speaking, he handed the babe to his sobbing wife, who, with averted face, received the child, and after listening to her husband's farewell, hurriedly quitted the apartment. When she was gone and Sir Common had said good-bye to his brother, he prostrated himself before his mother, and, in broken accents, bade her adieu.

The aged lady listened with unmoved countenance, and, counselling him to remember her advice, accompanied him to the porch and watched his departure.

He last saw her standing in the door-way regarding him affectionately.

Sir Common hastened from the place, being desirous of quickly returning to his duty, and thus banishing the sad thoughts that filled his soul.

About noon, when he had travelled nearly eighteen miles, he seated himself in the shade of a tree and opened his luncheon-box, in which he found the rice-cakes and food prepared by his mother. Taking a cake in his hand, he reverently lifted it to his forehead, then proceeded to partake of the repast, at the conclusion of which one rice-cake remained in the receptacle.

" What can I do with this ? " he mused. " If I keep it until night it will be spoiled and I cannot throw away her gift."

He glanced about him and noticed a pigeon's nest in the fork of a tree above his head, seeing which he placed the cake in a suitable spot and presently had the pleasure of beholding the pigeons feed their brood with his offering.

Sir Common watched their actions with a dreamy curiosity, his mind being preoccupied with thoughts of those who were far away. He was awakened from his reverie by the noise of the young birds clamoring for the food, which they devoured as fast as the old ones could procure it, the parents never once swallowing a morsel. Seeing this, Sir Common thought :

"Although the pigeon is a small bird, its parental instinct causes it to deny itself everything for its offspring. Do human beings think as much of their children? If I go to Yedo I shall either die fighting or by *hara-kiri*, and my life will be lost to my family. I have, in bidding farewell to my mother, been guilty of a grave falsehood. When all is over and she becomes acquainted with my deceit, she will most surely say 'Though I have thought so much of my son, his affection for me was so slight that he did not hesitate to deceive me,' and will feel displeased and lament. I have made a great mistake."

These reflections caused him to feel very unhappy, and prevented him from resuming his journey.

"I must return to her," he said. "I will reveal the true motive of my visit to Yedo and bid her farewell in a proper manner."

He then rose and retraced his steps, reaching home about sun-set.

Having allayed the apprehensions of his wife and brother by stating he had forgotten an important matter, he went to his mother s chamber and narrated the circumstances that had influenced him to revisit her, then said in a husky voice :

" I thoroughly feel my wickedness in confessing the truth at this late hour. It is as you have suspected; I am going to Yedo for the purpose of avenging the death of our honored lord. Sir Big-rock and others of the clan have vowed to accomplish this act of duty; therefore it will be impossible for me to visit you again. You are my only parent and I am conscious I ought to live with you and do my utmost to make your life happy, yet I cannot forget the grace of our late lord. How am I to fulfil both my loyal and filial duties ? I pray you will put your ungrateful and unworthy son out of your heart."

The lady listened with a delighted expression and gently replied

" You lovingly tried to conceal the truth from me, yet I was not for a moment deceived. Now that you have spoken frankly, my heart is rejoiced. My son, do your duty to our lord. That is the first thing a *samurai* should consider. Remember, your brother will be with me to comfort my last years. I am perfectly satisfied. Even had I no other son, you would have to keep your word and leave an untarnished name to your child. You could not, in any way. more perfectly fulfil your obligation to me than by acting thus. Dismiss me from your thoughts and concentrate your whole mind upon your duty. We will now drink a farewell cup."

She procured *saké* and entertained him, never by word or look showing the least indication of her grief.

When Sir Common had somewhat mastered his grief, he reverently opened the letter and read.

Chap. xxi, p. 165.

Sir Common, overjoyed with her loyalty of spirit, talked with her until nearly midnight, when they retired to their respective apartments.

At day-break he rose and waited outside his mother's room, knowing it was her custom to be up before the rest of the household. The hours passed and the sun mounted high into the heavens, yet there was no sign of her being awake. His wife came and went, and glanced at him uneasily, still he did not notice her or appear to observe the affectionate demonstrations of their child, who alternately peeped round the door-way at his papa and clamored for his grandmother.

At the hour of the dragon (8 A.M.), Sir Common, unable any longer to bear the suspense, entered his parent's chamber, and, to his horror and grief, discovered she was dead. By her pillow was a letter, stained with the life-blood of the noble and courageous lady.

" Brother! wife!" he cried, " come hither and see what mother has done for my sake !"

Total-three and Cloth hurried into the room, and when Sir Common had somewhat mastered his grief, he reverently opened the letter and read :

" I leave you a few words. My dear son, your kindness and affection toward me are beyond my poor expression. That you should come back the distance of eighteen miles, thinking of your mother, is only a slight evidence of your love for me. How happy is the woman who possesses such a son! After I parted from you I thought over your position, and saw that my duty is as clear as yours. You must go to the attack unfettered by any concern about me. Were a thought of that kind to enter your mind, your fortitude might forsake you, and you might afford the enemy a chance to behold the inside of your helmet. I am old and my life can well be spared. I joyfully end it in order to free you from anxiety, that you may die the death of a *samurai*. My son, I precede you to the land of shadows. Look upon Sir Kira not only as the enemy of our honored lord, but also as the executioner of your mother, and set an example of heroism to your comrades. Knowing you will surely do this, I die contented, and, smiling upon the knife, hasten to sever the thread of my existence. My last farewell to Total-three, to dear little Fusa Bo, to Cloth and to you, my dear son.

" MOTHER."

When Sir Common had read this he cried like a child at the top of his voice, after awhile observing

" There are many sons who do not fulfil their filial duties, but none so wicked as I. Had I foreseen this I would not have returned. Indeed, I have done the most foolish thing imaginable. How can I ever forget the noble example set me by my mother! A thousand times be accursed the wretch who caused all this misery!"

His brother and wife united with him in lamenting the death of their parent, and by turns embraced the inanimate form.

Grief, though natural, will not restore the dead to life ; so Sir Common, after having buried his mother with all honors and spent fourteen days in mourning at her tomb, bade farewell to his wife, child and brother, and, returning to Kioto, presented himself to Sir Big-rock, who, saluting him, said ;

"Well, Sir Common, you have been absent longer than you promised, moreover, you do not look as usual. Have you been sick ? "

" No, Sir Big-rock, there is nothing the matter with me. Unhappily, I have lost my honored mother. I disregarded the usual limit of mourning and returned as soon as possible."

" I regret to hear of your bereavement. Did your honorable mother die suddenly ? "

Sir Common related all that had occurred, even reading the letter, which so moved Sir Big-rock that the tears trickled down his cheeks, and he exclaimed

"Ah! the loyal heart of the *samurai* woman! Your honored mother is like the noble parent of Sir Straight-grove. Their united names will be reverently remembered by posterity. Those courageous ladies make us men blush with shame. I can well imagine your grief and that of your family. All this misery is the result of the meanness and wickedness of Sir Kira—the death of our lord, the sufferings of our clan—how can I express myself! The time of retribution is at hand. When you arrive in Yedo you may freely communicate my plans to our comrades, then wait for the day when we shall be able to return the sacred charge entrusted to me by our honored chief."

Sir Common, encouraged by Sir Big-rock's words, banished his sorrow, and, having stayed one day in Kioto, started for Yedo.

CHAPTER XXII.

MR. NOBLE-PLAIN.

"A glittering grain of gold is seen amid a hundred million particles of sand.
The humble garb of the peasant often covers a noble heart."

At the sign of the Heaven Stream (milky way) in the town of Sakai, near the seaport of Osaka, dwelt a man named Noble-plain, who, during the lifetime of Lord Morning-field, lived by supplying the clan of Ako with arms and other equipments. Upon hearing of the misfortune that had overtaken his employer, he hastened to the castle and sought an interview with Sir Big-rock, whom he thus addressed:

" Sir Chief-councillor, though only a *chonin* (literally street-people, a class including citizens, artizans and peasants), my heart is heavy with the calamity that has befallen my gracious patron, and I desire to do something to prove my gratitude for the many kindnesses I have received at his hands. Oh, that I were a *samurai*! even were my rations no more than a

handful of rice, I could then join in your noble enterprise and die an honorable death.   As it is, I know
not what to do."

Sir Big-rock listened with pleasure, and replied :

" Your generous devotion will gratify our dead chief.
Be patient and await the time when you will receive a
communication from me.   I have long been aware of
your honesty and fidelity, and will some day call upon
you to render us an important service."

" Sir Chief-councillor, I am henceforth at your command.   My fortune, my life,—all I possess is at your
disposal.   Be it to-morrow or ten years hence, you
will find me in the same mind.   Your words have
comforted my heart.   I shall look forward for the moment to arrive when you will avail yourself of my
humble aid."

He then took his leave and returned to Sakai.

The years passed, and, like the rest of the world,
Noble-plain heard strange stories concerning the behavior of Sir Big-rock, notwithstanding which he was
always expecting a summons from the Chief-councillor.

In October, 1701, a few days after the departure of
Sir Common for Yedo, a messenger entered the merchant's store and said :

" Are you Mr. Noble-plain ? "

" That is my name.   What can I do for you ? "

The new-comer approached him and whispered ;

" Would you like to earn a large sum of money ?

1 perceive your shop is not so well stocked as formerly and that you have only one assistant. Surely business must be very bad with you? "

The proprietor sighed and answered :

" Since the death of my noble patron my affairs have become all of a heap. I shall be most happy to better my condition."

"That is good. The service I require is a very easy one. You have heard of Sir Kira, late master of ceremonies to the Sho-gun. He wishes you to supply him with some arms."

Noble-plain's eyes flashed and he ground his teeth with rage, then exclaimed

" You dog! how dare you propose such a thing to me. Quit this place or I will kick you out."

The stranger, instead of complying with this command, drew a letter from his bosom and handed it to the merchant, saying :

" Before I go, I desire you will read this."

Noble-plain glanced at the superscription and saw that the communication was from Yamashina, and the bearer was designated as Temple-cliff. He opened the note and read as follows :

" An old employer desires to see you at your earliest convenience. He is about to engage in business, and wishes to give you a little commission.

" PEACEFUL-VALLEY,
" of Yamashina."

The overjoyed merchant prostrated himself before the messenger, and, after returning thanks, invited him to enter his private apartment, where he regaled him with *saké* and fish."

That night the two men started for Yamashina, and on the following morning Noble-plain presented himself to Sir Big-rock, who said :

" You must excuse the trick played by Temple-cliff. I am compelled to test even those whom I deem most faithful. I hear you are very poor, therefore am rejoiced to know, though you have lost your fortune, you still remember the goodness of your late patron."

" Sir Chief-councillor," replied the merchant, "it is true I have but little left, still what there is, is at your service."

Sir Big-rock produced a paper which he handed him, saying

"Enclosed you will find a list of certain articles I require delivered to the care of the chief-priest of the Spring-hill Temple in the High-rope district of Yedo. I wish you to attend to this matter at once, and will leave the details to your judgment; merely remarking that absolute secrecy must be observed in the matter."

Noble-plain opened the document, and after scanning it, said :

" I understand what you want and will have everything at the place you mention before the snow begins to fly. The uniforms I will procure in Yedo, also the bamboo pins and pocket writing materials. I will start at once and you may rely upon your secret being well kept. Sir Chief-councillor, I am overjoyed at receiving this commission; I feel as though I were walking upon the air."

" With regard to funds," said Sir Big-rock,—

" I shall sell my stock and business," replied the merchant. " Have no apprehension on the score of money, I will attend to that."

Sir Big-rock sent for a package which he gave to the man; remarking as he did so

" Here are two hundred *rio*; if this sum be insufficient, call upon Sir Common, who is living at the Three-springs grocery store, near the residence of Sir Kira, in Yedo. He will hand you any further funds you may require."

Noble-plain took his leave, and returning to his home, informed his wife that he was going to the province of Bingo, then secretly set out post-haste for Yedo.

A few days after the merchant's departure, Sir Big-rock received the following communication from the capital :

" The late beautiful weather has been very favorable for eeling and the Associated Anglers have been out early and late. Yesterday we tried our fortune in the old stream, containing the big eel. Although we searched every nook and corner we failed to get sight of him.   At last, toward the evening, we learned that he had quitted his usual retreat and taken refuge beneath the shade of a tall cedar.   You remember the saying of Confucius   'It is foolish to go to a tree in order to catch fish.'   This case will prove an exception to the rule.   Your experience as an angler will enable you to suggest some means by which we can secure the monster.

" Associated Anglers."

After Sir Big-rock had read this, he laughed to himself and exclaimed :

" So, Sir Kira has left his house and sought refuge with his son Lord Upper-cedar.   When I join the Assiated Anglers we will capture that slippery eel."

CHAPTER XXIII.

SIR BIG-ROCK DEPARTS FOR YEDO.

Among the celebrated ladies of the clan of Ako was Mrs. Brilliant, wife of Sir Hatchet, who, like him, was a poet, and wrote many verses that have been preserved to this day. She was famous for her virtues, wisdom and talents, and possessed a noble and loyal soul. Gentle in manner, obedient to her husband, and kind to her mother-in-law, she not only managed her household affairs with consummate ability, but found time to continue her studies in Japanese and Chinese literature, in addition to which her whole heart was in the conspiracy, and she made her house the rendezvous of the loyal leaguers.

During the lifetime of Lord Morning-field, Sir Hatchet was the governor of his chief's residence in Kioto, and after the noble's death, the poet continued to reside in that city, where he earned his living by instructing pupils in the art of composing elegant stanzas.

Toward the end of October, when the tempests had

stripped the autumnal garb from the trees, an epidemic appeared in Kioto, and among its first victims were the mother of Sir Hatchet, and his daughter, Miss Plum. While the sleeves of the mourners were yet wet with tears, Sir Hatchet was instructed to depart for Yedo. Mrs. Brilliant received the news with heroic fortitude, and bade adieu to her husband as though he was going to a festival, congratulating him that he would soon accomplish what they both so greatly desired.

Brave and wise woman, where can we find her equal ?

Sir Hatchet was accompanied by Sir Big-rock, Jr., and, in order to deceive their enemies, they left Kioto under the pretence of making a pilgrimage to the shrine of the goddess Amaterasu Omi-kami, in the province of Ise (the Mecca of believers in the Shinto faith).

On their way the poet delighted his companion by describing the objects and places of historic interest, which he made the subjects of impromptu verses.

After crossing a river, that in the morning sun sent up a heavy mist, he observed :

" As I emerge from the Kamo, I take with me the vapor of the stream."

At Shiga, he said :

" Lonely and cold stands the solitary pine-tree on the shore of Shiga.

" So lives a person (meaning his wife) at home."

Sir Hatchet glanced across the glittering water on his right, and said : "I see, reflected upon the bosom of the bay the snow-clad peak of Fuji-san "

These poems showed the young man, that while Sir Hatchet was apparently unconcerned, he was thinking of the beloved one whom he had left in Kioto.

When the travelers reached the town of Kanagawa, they halted for a day to celebrate the majority of Sir Big-rock, Jr., who, that morning, had his forelock shaven, and received the military name of Good-gold.

Upon the following day, as they were proceeding on their journey, the fog that had for the previous twenty-four hours enveloped Fuji-yama, suddenly lifted, noticing which, Sir Hatchet looked across the glittering water upon his right, and said :

" I see, reflected upon the bosom of the bay, the snow-clad peak of Fuji-san."

His companion, hearing this, turned, and glancing at the mountain, joyfully exclaimed :

" Oh, happy omen ! Fuji-yama salutes me on attaining my majority ! May it thus greet me upon the morning of my accomplishing the desire of my heart ! "

Toward evening they arrived at their destination, and were warmly welcomed by their fellow conspirators. From that time Sir Big-rock, Jr. assumed a position of responsibility, and assisted in the task of watching the enemy.

Soon after Sir Hatchet and his companion departed for Yedo, Sir Big-rock began to examine his papers and arrange them in order, like one who prepares for death. When he had completed this task, his maid-servant,

" Honorable master, is it true you have decided that I shall not accompany you ? "

" Yes," was the reply. " I require a responsible person here to receive any of my friends who may call. You will, in my absence, take charge of the house."

This delighted the old man, who saluted his master, and retired with an important air.

That evening Sir Big-rock proceeded to the temple of the Snow-clad Pine, and received the *sambo* and white-wood box.

Early the next morning, the neighbors saw the Chief-councillor and his two servants quit the house, behind them being a hired coolie laden with their baggage.

"I said you might begin to write about five days after my departure, and thinking there might be a letter from you at the address I named, yesterday made inquiry, but found none had arrived. Are you still at our home? If you are lonely, why not take some one to live with you or go to reside with a friend? Oh! how I pity you, knowing you must miss the beautiful objects of art and the furniture to which you have been so long accustomed and which you sold to defray my expenses hither! You must feel in the absence of those things as though the house had grown larger. I dare say you also miss the many callers who visited us when we were together. I fancy I can see you sitting lonely and comfortless. I pray you will endeavor to conquer your grief, as I am trying to do mine.

"Has Wisteria-three returned the money I loaned him? You had better urge him to do·this. I hope Wisteria-help has paid the principal and interest due me. Be careful not to be cheated or robbed.

"Yesterday, the first monthly anniversary of our mother's death, I felt very sad, not being able to visit her tomb, so, in order to disperse my melancholy, called upon our adopted son, who gave me some good *saké*, and comforted me by saying you would do everything necessary and pay the priests for praying for the repose of our dear parent's soul.

"I resume my pen to-day, the 29th November, having written the foregoing whenever I had a few moments to spare.

"Last night I received your letters of the 15th and
16th inst., which gave me great happiness.   I seemed,
while perusing them, to be talking with you, and read
them slowly, so as to get the full sense of every
word.

"You say you still have the pain in your left ribs ;
that you cannot sleep on that side ; also that your
pulse is weak.   You have done well to consult Dr.
Village-cottage.   Remembering what you have suffered, I am not surprised you are sick.   Sorrow always
produces diseases of the body.   You must not allow
yourself to grieve so much ; you are friendless enough,
and it is important you should take care of your health.
Your answer to Wisteria-help, the district registrar,
was perfectly correct.   If he troubles you with further
enquiry, tell him to wait until the end of the year,
when he will hear from me.   I am not astonished there
are many rumors with regard to Sir Big-rock, and it
pleases me to hear none of the people suspect the
truth.

"I am glad you visited the tomb of our mother
and distributed the alms ; also that the tomb-stone was
finished and placed in position, and the stone-cutter's
bill was so reasonable.

"Although our separation is the result of a determination made long ago, yet we both sorely feel the sadness it has brought about.   You say, during the day
your occupation prevents you from dwelling too much
upon your misery, yet when night comes you cannot

sleep from thinking of me. My poor, dear wife, I feel
the same as you do. The saying, ' Not seeing is forgetting,' does not apply either to you or me. As the
days pass, the greater grows our sorrow ; still, if we
reason correctly, we will find each misfortune is a step
toward the attainment of wisdom. You already know
these things, yet, by reflecting upon them, will gradually learn the philosophy of human life, and thus soothe
your sorrow. Our duty is not to lament over what is
irreparable, but to bear the misfortunes inflicted upon
us by the gods ; yet, my dear wife, I pity you.

" You tell me you are pleased with my poems, especially that upon the Osaka Pass. I greatly admire
those enclosed in your letters. By the way, I hope
you will not give up composing verses, but will write
one whenever you have a spare moment and send it
to me. During my journey hither, I had little to disturb my mind and could think about verse-making ;
however, since my arrival here, I have been surrounded by visitors and have had little time for corre-
spondence.

" I am sorry to tell you bad news. The fact is, Sir
Kira is hiding somewhere, and, like a badger, does
not give any sign of his whereabouts. I hope, now
that every arrangement has been made, our enemy
will not slip through our fingers.

The younger members of our party are full of courage. Sir Lucky-field, Sir Common, Sir Unconquerable, Sir Early-crop and myself being the seniors, are in hourly consultation and arrange everything for the others. Yesterday the theatres opened for the winter season, and the boys, including our son, took a holiday and went to witness the performances. We live in bachelor style, the juniors doing the house-work and waiting upon us at meals. They treat us very kindly. We all have nick-names. They call me 'doctor,' saying I have a forelock growing like a physician s. The sleeves and linings of my clothes are beginning to wear, but, remembering I shall only be here for a little while longer, I have let them go. To-day our son, noticing a large rent in my coat, insisted upon sewing it up, and I allowed him to have his way. During the night I put on all my garments, as it is very cold here. You said I had better take another suit with me, I am exceedingly sorry I did not follow your advice.

" Yesterday I went to a store to buy some geese, and seeing they were very nice and reasonable in price, bought an extra one, which I have had boned and salted. You will receive it in a box with this letter. There is no necessity for you to soak it, as it is only slightly corned. Make it into soup, and when Dr. Valley-cottage calls, give him some of it with *saké.*

" Since writing the above I have removed to the house of Big-rock Jr., which is some distance from where our son is staying.

" Remember, my beloved wife, I am well in health, so try to comfort yourself. You may at any moment receive the welcome news.

" I have written this letter under circumstances of great difficulty. You will hear from me up to the last moment.

" November the 30th,

   " To my dear Brilliant,

      " HATCHET."

CHAPTER XXV

THE MEETING IN THE SPRING-HILL TEMPLE.

" Our most fervent vows of vengence are made in the peaceful abodes of the gods."

The leaguers knew Sir Big-rock was in Yedo, but few of them saw him, though all felt the power of his presence. From the first to the tenth of December, everyone was actively employed in endeavoring to discover the whereabouts of Sir Kira, spite of which they were unsuccessful, their enemy having vanished like a cloud. They haunted the vicinity of his son's residence and even penetrated into the mansion, yet all they could learn was that he had quitted the place for parts unknown. The younger of the conspirators became greatly excited, finding which Sir Big-rock summoned them to meet him in the Spring-hill Temple.

At the hour of the Fox (10 P.M.) on the 11th of December, a number of men stealthily approached the sacred building, and by midnight the leaguers were all assembled in a large apartment behind the main altar. The priests guarded every entrance and took care that

184

no one should surprise their visitors. A dead silence reigned in the dimly-lighted hall, and the conspirators, who knelt in two rows, eagerly awaited the arrival of their chief. As the midnight hour was struck upon the great bell, Sir Big-rock slowly entered the hall. In his hands he bore the *sambo* and white pine box, which, having placed upon the *tokonoma*, he respectfully saluted. After returning the bows of his comrades, he directed Sir Common to call the roll.

Forty-seven ronins answered " Here."

The flickering, red light of the candles feebly illuminated the apartment, and little could be seen save the pale faces of the clansmen, who, advancing close to their leader, crouched in a semicircle about the *sambo*, the contents of which were unknown to most of them.

Sir Big-rock remained for a moment with his head bowed, as though in deep thought, then, gazing upon them, said :

" Brothers, three years ago our beloved lord committed this legacy to my charge. Since that time some of his followers have proved faithless to their plighted words ; those we leave to the vengeance of the gods and the contempt of their fellow-men. We, who are here assembled, have been thrice tried and have waited patiently, bearing everything that we might some day be in a position to perform our too-long deferred duty. Our enemy, powerful and vigilant, had to be deceived into believing that we were disloyal and many things had to be done ere we were prepared to strike the blow. I yesterday received information that Sir Kira, disbelieving in our devotion to our honored chief, is about to return to his home, and that on the anniversary of the death of our beloved lord he will give a feast to his friends. On that night he shall cease to live. We care not how closely he may be guarded. Be there ten thousand men at his command, we will cut our way through them and accomplish our aim."

This speech was received with murmurs of approval, the conspirators grasping the hilts of their swords, as though eager to attack their enemy.

Sir Big-rock removed the lid of the box, and took from it a package wrapped in a purple cloth. After raising this to his forehead, he opened the folds and revealed a blood-stained dirk, exclaiming as he exhibited it to the assembly:

"This is the weapon that shall end Sir Kira's life. I swear by the hundred million gods never to leave his residence until our duty is performed."

The conspirators, aroused to frenzy by his words, pressed forward, and reverently touching the dirk, joined in his vow; then, after receiving instructions as to their places of rendezvous on the night of the 14th, silently departed to their lodgings, leaving him kneeling, and regarding the legacy of his chief, in which attitude he remained till daybreak.

Before quitting the temple he gave audience to

Noble-plain, the contractor, and inspected the uniforms and accoutrements provided by the latter, and that done, retired to his lodging in a house opposite the residence of Sir Kira.

CHAPTER XXVI.

SIR SHELL AND HIS FAMILY

" At the call of duty, the *samurai* bids farewell to those who are dear to him.

" Though the face be calm and resolute, the heart may be surcharged with sorrow."

" My dear husband, are you going to Original-village to-day?"

" Yes, my love, it will never do for me to remain idle. If I were to die suddenly and we had nothing laid by, how you would suffer."

The speakers were Sir Shell and his wife, Mrs. Home, who had been married nearly three years. In the ardor of his wooing he had not reflected upon the consequences of tying the thread of love, however, after their union, when he had time for reflection, he thought

" I know I have acted indiscreetly, still what could I do? I tenderly love my wife, yet cannot prove faithless to my lord, and when the time comes, must tear myself away. The past cannot be recalled. Home is young and attractive, and will, I hope, find some one to console her for my loss."

This comforted him until their son was born, when he discovered the grievousness of his mistake and found he had two helpless beings dependent on him. Thus, while the advent of the babe was a source of great happiness to the mother, the sight of the little one filled the father's heart with pity and sorrow, and he secretly reproached himself with being the cause of the misery he knew must soon overtake them.

On the morning of the 12th of December, when Sir Shell was proceeding home from the Spring-hill Temple, he determined to inform his wife of their approaching separation. Upon beholding her, his courage failed, so, after eating his breakfast, he went out for the day to watch the residence of Sir Kira.

As he quitted the house, his wife thought to herself:

"What is the trouble that has come upon my husband? He goes out late in the evening and returns at all hours, and is often moody and thoughtful. I wonder whether I have done anything to make him so unhappy? Even the smiles of our little one have ceased to attract his attention."

That evening after sunset, Mrs. Home lighted the charcoal in the fire-bowl, and seating herself near her work-box, began to sew upon a garment for her husband. Her babe, Also-five-boy, was sleeping peacefully on a rug by her side, with his arms extended and

his head resting on a cushion, near him being his toys,
—a mottled dog, a rattle, and a rag doll.   While she
was thus employed, Sir Shell entered, and after depositing his sword in the *katana-kake* (sword-rack), seated
himself by the fire-bowl, and having lighted his pipe,
said

" Dear Home, there is something I have long desired to tell you."

" What is it ? " she enquired, glancing anxiously at
him.

He thought for awhile and replied :

" It is necessary I should go upon a long journey.   I
may have to start very soon."

" My dear husband, I am ready to accompany you
at any moment.   Also-five-boy is now old enough to
travel and will not be any trouble.   Really, the news
delights me.   I hope we are going to Ako, as I would
like to visit your native place."

Sir Shell laid down his pipe, and folding his arms,
said in a gentle voice :

" My dear Home, I am not going to Ako.   The
journey I am about to make is not a matter of one or
two hundred miles, but a long and tiresome one, and
there are many perils to be encountered on the road.
Indeed, I may never return alive."

" Still I would prefer to accompany you," she
pleaded.

" That will be impossible," he said.   " I have
thought it all over and decided it is best for you and

As he watched her and their sleeping babe, scalding tears trickled down his cheeks and dropped upon his hands.

Chap. xxvi, p. 191.

our son to remain here. Surely you do not desire to risk his life? It will be bad enough for you to part with me. No, no, my dear wife, you remain here and take care of our boy while I go to better our fortune."

He then produced a package of money which Sir Big-rock had given him that afternoon, and handing it to her, continued :

" This sum will last you for a long time."

The agitated woman burst into tears and covering her face with her sleeves sobbed convulsively.

Sir Shell, who felt as though his heart were torn to pieces, regarded her pityingly without being able to reply. He realized, for the first time, the full force of the sacrifice he was about to make, and as he watched her and their sleeping babe, scalding tears trickled down his cheeks and dropped upon his hands.

After awhile the agonized woman made a great effort and said, as she pointed to the child

" My honorable husband, I understand all. You wish to cast me off. I, who have brought you nothing but anxiety and misery, I feared this was coming and have no reproaches to make ; but, even though you do not love me, beg you will think of our child, and put off your intention until he is old enough to remember your face. Oh. bear with me for his sake and do not let him suffer for my faults ! You tell me you have to go upon a long journey, that is your kind pretext for putting me away. Alas, alas, that we ever met in the restaurant at Asakusa ! Would I had died before that day, then I should never have known this great sorrow! Were you a cruel husband I might find comfort in your decision, but you have always been most kind and affectionate. When this child was born I felt doubly happy in believing he would be the means of strengthening our love."

She threw herself at his feet, and after uttering a despairing cry, exclaimed

" O honorable husband! I pray you to put an end to our lives! I cannot exist without you!"

The distracted man bowed his head and was utterly unable to reply. He suffered untold agony in the conflict between his love and duty, and in the prospect of leaving his dear ones for the journey to the unknown; and, biting his lips, felt as though he would have to break his loyal vow.

The babe awoke and crawling toward his mother peered up at her face; then, hearing her sobs, began to cry piteously, thus adding to their sorrow.

Sir Shell, no longer able to bear the sight, hastily arose, and quitting the house, paced the street, leaving his wife to comfort the babe.

The hours passed until the distant sound of the temple bell announced the arrival of midnight, when Sir Shell crept back to his home and halting in the porch heard Mrs. Home singing:

" *Nen neko okorori nen neko yo.*
Obo san yoiko da nen neko yo ;
Obo san ga nen neko shita ato dé,

Yama saka koyete ikimashite,
Aka no omamma ni toto soyete
Oriko na obo san, no mezameni agema sho."

TRANSLATION.

Sleep! Sleep! my good baby, sleep!

While my gentle baby slumbers, I will go over the mountains and through the valleys and fetch some red-bean rice and fish!

When my clever baby awakens, I will feed him with the red-bean rice and fish!

I will go over the mountains and through the valleys!

Sleep! Sleep! my good baby, sleep!

The husband listened with heaving breast and troubled face; then, as the sad air died away, quietly entered his dwelling and stretched himself upon his bed.

At last the angel of sleep threw his shadow over the abode of sorrow, and, for a brief space, caused the inmates to forget their unhappiness.

CHAPTER XXVII.

SIR BIG-ROCK MAKES REPARATION TO HIS WIFE.

"Judge no one until the grass has grown upon his grave.
Only the gods know the secrets of our souls."

On the morning of the 13th of December, Sir Big-rock rose early, and after devoting several hours to writing, summoned his servants, Happy-seven and Left-six, whom he thus addressed

" The time has arrived when I no longer require your services. I desire you will both proceed to Rich-cliff and take with you these letters and this package, which you will personally deliver into the hands of my father-in-law."

The men, having been in constant attendance upon him, were aware of the conspiracy and had hoped to die with their employer. Happy-seven bowed humbly and said

" Honorable master, we pray you will allow us to remain with you to the end. We desire to attend you upon your last journey. This is the determination we made long ago."

194

When the men heard this they wept, and begged he would reconsider his decision.

Chap. xxvii, p. 195.

Sir Big-rock listened attentively and replied :

" I will be frank with you. The hour is at hand when the clansmen will carry out their long-cherished plan. It is impossible for me to grant your prayer, as none but the members of the league will be permitted to join in the attack. If you wish to serve me, do as I request, and devote the remainder of your lives to attending upon my family."

When the men heard this they wept and begged he would re-consider his decision, and it was with difficulty he restrained them from ending their lives there and then. At last, Left-six dried his tears and said in a choking voice :

" Honorable master, we will obey. I see it is not fit for such common fellows as we are to take part in your glorious enterprise."

" Yes," said Happy-seven, " as long as we live we will remember your goodness, and serve your honorable family as faithfully as we have done you."

They then received their wages and the letters and package, and set out for their destination, feeling sure that the time of attack was close at hand.

Sir Big-rock's communications were addressed respectively to his father-in-law, his wife and his children. The first was a long epistle in which the *samurai* narrated the history of the conspiracy, and commended his family to the guardianship of his father-in-law. The third was to his sons, giving, among other things, a list of books he desired they

should read, also minute instructions for their guidance.

The second letter was to his wife, Mrs. Stone, and
read as follows

" By Happy-seven and Left-six, whom I now dismiss from my service and commend to your care, I
send you a few lines.

" In the first place I ask you, my dear and honored
wife, to forgive me for the apparently brutal conduct
with which I treated you.   Oh! how I suffered that
cold December morning, when my sense of duty compelled me to tear myself away from you and put upon
you the stigma of divorce !   It was my only means of
deceiving our enemy, and nothing I have done has
been so effectual in blinding him as to my real designs.
You have, in bearing this injustice, done your duty as
a wife and member of the clan, and your sacrifice will
be fully recognized by our honored chief.   My dear
love, though I shall never see you again in this life,
my spirit will be ever present, watching over your welfare and that of our children.

" I can now face death without a pang, knowing you
will understand what has hereto appeared unnatural in
my behavior.   Admirable wife and noble mother, your
name will be remembered longer than my own, for you
have made three offerings at the shrine of loyalty—
your husband, your son, and yourself.

" I now bid you a temporary farewell.   Oh, wife of
my heart ! when the duty to our lord is accomplished

and I have departed to the land of shadows, think of me as tenderly as you have done during my life, and when the time comes for you to travel the Lonely-road, rest assured I will be waiting to greet you at the termination of your journey.

" I leave the education of our sons entirely to you, and hope my poor example will teach them to live and die loyal men and to be true to their duties.

" Herewith I send you a letter from our brave son, Good-gold.

" To my dear wife, Stone.

" BIG-ROCK."

CHAPTER XXVIII.

THE MISSION OF SIR HAWK'S-GROVE.

"Snow was in the air and on the house-tops, and the geese flying high overhead could not be seen by the passers-by."

On the morning of the 14th of December the wind suddenly shifted to the north, thick white clouds piled up upon the horizon, and soon the air became filled with feathery particles of snow, which continued to descend until the city of Yedo was covered with a white veil.

Few people ventured into the streets, and the cold gradually became intense.

Toward noon a *samurai*, dressed in a rain-coat, entered a buckwheat-vermicelli restaurant at the western end of the Two-provinces Bridge, and after saluting the proprietor, said :

"Mr. Long-time, I have come to ask a favor and to say I am about to bid you farewell. First of all let me have a drink of *saké* and some of your famous vermicelli. This snow-storm is enough to chill one to the marrow."

The propietor ordered a servant to bring the refreshments, then, squatting by his friend, said :

" Mr. Hawk's-grove, or rather, pardon me, Sir Hawk s-grove, for I perceive you are no longer a merchant. What do you mean by saying you are about to bid me farewell ? Has your tobacco business proved an unfortunate speculation ? "

" Yes, somewhat," replied the *samurai.* " The fact is I have spent much to get very little, and the price of rice being high, found it hard to earn a living. I have been in consultation with some of my former comrades, who, like myself, are *ronin.* We have had an offer from a Prince, related to our old master, and have accepted positions in his service."

" That's good," said the restaurant-keeper. " You remember the old proverb : ' One cannot make a merchant out of a *samurai.*' Still I am sorry you are going away, as after knowing you for three years I regret being obliged to end our acquaintance. When do you start ? "

" Not until to-night. During the day the roads are soft ; however, when the moon rises the frost increases, and the traveling will be more pleasant; besides, as there are over twenty in our party, we shall not fear the attacks of highwaymen. The favor I have to ask is this. We intended to assemble in my house and take supper, but my place is too small to accommodate such a large party. I have come to ask if you will entertain us here."

" Certainly," answered Mr. Long-time. " That is my business. Do you wish me to prepare anything in addition to our usual bill of fare ? "

" Yes," said Sir Hawk's-grove, taking a sum of money from his pocket-book. " I will leave this amount in your hands. Please have ready sufficient *saké*, rice, fish and vermicelli to satisfy twenty-five hungry persons."

The proprietor received the coins, saying

" Although no advance payment is needed from a friend, I will keep this. How late do you desire the repast ready ? "

" By the hour of the Fox (10 P. M.)," answered the *samurai*. " By that time all your regular customers will have taken their departure ? "

" Yes," sadly replied the other, " between ourselves, my business is not flourishing ; so, to make up for the deficiency in my receipts, I have been renting my rooms to *haikai* (verse-making) parties, who seldom stay beyond the hour of the Hog (8 P. M.). There is no fear of disturbing my guests ; you will have the whole house to yourselves."

When they had chatted for awhile, Sir Hawk's-grove quitted the restaurant, drew his rain-coat tightly about him, and pulled his broad-brimmed hat well over his eyes, so as to shield his face from the blinding snow. He crossed the Two-provinces Bridge, and entering the street at the rear of Sir Kira's residence, proceeded to a tea-house, where he engaged rooms for a second party, telling the same story he' had related to the keeper of the vermicelli restaurant.

Having accomplished this mission he sauntered toward the back gate of the noble's mansion, and taking shelter in a road-side refreshment stall, ordered some tea, at the same time secretly watching all who entered the opposite portal.

"Ah!" laughingly exclaimed the one-eyed patriarch who kept the stall, "this is like old times ; I shall be very busy this evening. The great Sir Kira is to entertain a number of his friends, and my kettles will be emptied many times."

The *samurai* pretended not to be interested, and the speaker, who repeatedly slapped his hands to keep himself warm, continued:

"Ah! there will be glorious doings in the mansion. They have made preparations for over a hundred guests. Sir Kira is a very good man. About an hour ago I saw his lacquered *norimono* enter yonder gateway."

The *ronin* handed him some money, then made the best of his way to the house where Sir Big-rock was staying. He informed the Chief-councillor of what he had heard, when the former said :

"Good, the wary eel has entered the trap."

CHAPTER XXIX.

SIR RED-FENCE AND HIS BOTTLE.

" Every one has a hobby, allow me then the ways of Nihon (to make verses).
Provided a man pays for his *saké*, it is no one's business how much he drinks."

Soon after Sir Hawk's-grove made his report to Sir Big-rock, and while the storm was raging furiously, a *samurai*, whose gait betokened he had taken more *saké* than was good for him, staggered along West Street in the district of Small-stone river. His face was red and his eyes had a wild look, still he appeared to know where he was going, and took great care to protect a large earthen bottle that was suspended from his girdle. Every few moments he would pause, raise the skirt of his rain-coat and ascertain if his treasure were safe, then mutter something about the storm and continue his zig-zag career.

This *samurai* was Sir Red-fence, who had a strange history. He was the younger brother of Sir Turf-ground, of the clan of Autumn-moon, and when quite young had been adopted by a family who acknowledged the Lord of Ako as their chief. Unfortunately, Sir Red-fence had a great weakness, an inordinate love for liquor, and was almost constantly under its influence. This failing greatly be-littled him in the eyes of strangers, notwithstanding which he had many times been employed by his lord to conduct negociations that required great tact and ability. Why was this? Because, even though Sir Red-fence were intoxicated and lying on the floor in a state of stupefaction, he would, at the summons of duty, instantly arise and perform faithfully whatever was entrusted to him, in addition to which he was very eloquent and possessed sound judgment, and in the capacity of ambassador to the princely families, had done his lord good service.

It had generally happened that when he set out upon one of these errands, he was suffering from indulgence in his favorite beverage, and although at first he would endeavor to preserve a dignified appearance, before he had gone a hundred yards he would drop the reins upon the neck of his horse and begin to nod, leaving the animal to go as it pleased and permitting it to crop the grass growing on the road-side. His attendants, shamed by the grins and remarks of the passers-by, would waken their master and respectfully caution him, when, without even opening his eyes, he would mutter :

" Well, well! I know all about it. I am very sleepy."

He would yawn and resume his slumbers until he

arrived in front of the residence of the *daimio* to whom
he was accredited and heard the loud announcement :
" An ambassador is at the gate ! "

From that instant he would become wide awake,
and by his dignity of manner command the admiration of the by-standers. He was like the man described in the old saying :

" Although sent in four directions at once, he would
still preserve the honor of his master."

Lord Morning-field had great regard for Sir Red-
fence, and would often praise him for his ability ; while
among the clansmen no one was more devoted to
their chief than this drunken *samurai.*

After Sir Red-fence became a *ronin* he continued
to indulge in his potations, and although he often
wanted rice, was seldom without liquor.

Having no regular income and being unable to gain
his living by any occupation, he depended upon his
brother, Sir Turf-ground, a good man, who, recollecting the last injunction of their father, not only furnished the prodigal with money but bought him good
clothes.

Unhappily this benevolence was of little benefit to
Sir Red-fence, for upon receiving a new suit, he
would sell it to the first purchaser of cast off garments
he met and invest the proceeds in drink.

His dissolute behavior, while grieving Sir Turf-
ground, never lessened the latter's affection, and he
continued to do everything in his power for the way-

ward man, who would haunt his house and amuse the servants with his drunken antics.

Whenever he made his appearance at his brother's establishment, the domestics, although they looked upon him as an unmitigated sot and good-for-nothing, would quit their work in order to listen to his witticisms and watch his comical tricks. This finally became such a nuisance and so seriously interfered with their occupations, that Sir Turf-ground began to wish his brother would visit him less frequently and the lady of the house positively refused to see her relative.

Such was Sir Red-fence, who, bad as he was, had many virtues.

The snow beat into his face and he from time to time was obliged to pause to take breath and ascertain his whereabouts.

" This wintery storm makes one feel as if stone-pins were being driven into one's flesh," he muttered, as he leaned against the side of a house. " I wonder where my brother's residence has gone to, surely it has not been blown away? Thanks to the gods, I have brought my bottle with me. Those at his establishment are usually empty."

His shabby garments, which were partly concealed by a red paper waterproof cloak, and his old straw rain-hat, which he wore athwart his visage, gave him a very disreputable appearance and he in no way resembled " one who remembers his master."

In a few moments he resumed his weary journey,

walking unconcernedly through the snow-drifts and puddles, until he reached the side gate of the mansion of Lord Autumn-moon.

After passing the porter, who was crouching over the fire-bowl in the lodge, he halted, and addressing his bottle as though it could understand him, said :

"The cold does not seem to affect you, my old fellow. Of the hundred medical remedies *saké* is the chief."

The porter waited until the visitor was out of hearing, then laughed and remarked to a companion who was sitting near him   "There goes Sir Red-fence and his bottle, both of them are full of *saké*."

"Would I were like them," replied the other.   " A. good, warm cup would not be amiss on such a cold afternoon.   I have heard Sir Red-fence has never tasted water "

" I wish I could say the same," growled the porter " I believe the gods supply some people with their drink.   Sir Red-fence always has a drop in his bottle."

The object of their remarks, who had assumed a more sober gait, strode across the enclosure and proceeding to the side door of his brother's residence, entered.   Upon beholding him, the two maids who were in the kitchen glanced at each other, and the elder quitted the apartment to inform her mistress of his arrival, while the younger, advancing a step or two, knelt, bowed and addressed him, saying :

" Sir Red-fence, you are welcome.   You must have felt very cold on your way."

The *samurai* threw aside his rain-coat and tore off his hat without untying the cords, then carefully placing his bottle upon the platform, seated himself near it and smiling at the attendant, replied :

" Girl, I thank you for your kind words, but, as you see, I am warmed with good *saké* and the cold does not trouble me. How is my brother? Is his health affected by this weather? Is he at home? "

" Sir Red-fence, my master is well. At the present moment he is at the mansion, assisting our prince to entertain some guests. I do not think he will return until late to-night.

" Very good. Tell me how my sister is ? "

At that moment the other servant re-entered the kitchen and said :

" Honorable sir, my mistress is indisposed. She begs you will excuse her from seeing you."

Sir Red-fence nodded, saying :

" Oh! this severe cold is quite too much for her. I hope she will soon recover."

He spoke indistinctly and the girls imperfectly understood what he said. After awhile he appeared to doze, noticing which the elder of the servants whispered to her companion

" I will go to my mistress and leave you to wait upon the honorable brother. You are not afraid of him, are you ? "

" Not in the least," she replied. " No one fears Sir Red-fence. He never harmed a woman in his life."

When the old servant had departed, the sleeper suddenly jerked himself upright and exclaimed :

" Let me have a cup."

" Of tea ? " she inquired.

" Girl ! you know I never drink it. I have too much respect for my nerves ! ' Here is some old *saké* which I have brought as a present for my dear brother. Before giving it to you, I will ascertain whether it has been poisoned."

The maid laughed behind her sleeve, and handing him a cup, said

" Honorable sir, shall I warm the *saké* for you ? "

" A thousand thanks," he replied. " I can do that for myself."

He filled the cup and emptied it, repeating the operation several times, while the girl regarded him with an astonished face. The bottle was quite large, and it took him some time to reduce its contents. When only a small quantity remained in the vessel, he shook it and said to the attendant

" There is too much poison in this *saké ;* still the few cups that remain will not do you girls any harm. Accept it from me and finish it before you go to bed."

The damsel received his gift in a hesitating manner and put it aside, after which the visitor rose, and thrusting his toe into the loop of his left clog, which during the conversation had dropped from his foot, said

" Honorable Sir, shall I warm the *saki* for you ? A thousand thanks," he replied, " I can do that for myself ! "

" Please be good enough to listen to what I am about to tell you, and faithfully repeat my words to my brother."

" Of course I will, Sir Red-fence."

" Very well, girl. Now listen, and tell him this : Since I became a *ronin* you have been most kind to me, for which I return my heartfelt thanks. My fondness for *saké* has caused you much anxiety and annoyance. I beg you will forgive my offences. At length I have procured employment under a western prince, with whom I am about to start for his province. I came here to say farewell, and am sorry enough to depart without seeing you. Rest assured, even should it happen that I die without again beholding your face, the remembrance of your brotherly kindnesses will ever remain in my heart."

At this point Sir Red-fence dropped a tear, but the girl did not notice it. He then moved toward the door, upon reaching which he turned and said

" Also tell him Hereafter and forever I will entreat the gods to make both you and my sister prosperous and happy."

Thus speaking, he placed his hand to his head, and missing his rain-hat returned to recover it, when he found that in pulling it off he had broken the cords. As he was about to envelope his head in a soiled handkerchief, the girl took a hat hanging upon the wall and handing it to him, said :

" Honorable sir, it storms too much for you to go

abroad with your head thus unprotected. This is my
master's hat ; take it and leave your own."

" I thank you. I must now be off. I hope you girls
will have a happy New Year."

He hastily retired, and conquering his sorrowful reflections, hurried through the snow. Within an hour
he was perfectly sober, and had joined the conspirators
assembled at the grocery-store of the Three-springs.

Soon after Sir Red-fence quitted his brother's house
Sir Turf-ground returned, and on receiving the message from his wife, said

" I regret not to have seen him. He has remained
away so long I feared something had befallen the poor
fellow. I understand the end of the year is at hand,
and he requires my assistance. I am glad to hear he
has at last taken service, though it is a strange time
for a prince to proceed to his province. I suppose the
girl did not comprehend my brother's words, and suspect he is about to depart upon some important errand.
This is bitterly cold weather for a journey. I hope he
will not meet with any accident. My dear wife, I am
really very uneasy about him."

Had Sir Turf-ground known the truth he would
have felt proud of his relative, he hoping that Sir Red-
fence and the rest of the clansmen of Ako would some
day avenge the death of their lord. As it was, he
thought only of the profligate, and with difficulty restrained his tears.

His wife noticing his emotion, placed a repast before him, and bade the servant bring some *saké*. The girl produced the bottle left by Sir Red-fence, and minutely described how he had partaken of its contents.

Sir Turf-ground smiled sadly, and when the maid had retired, remarked to his wife

" Red-fence has only one fault—when there is a bottle near him he forgets everything else. I believe his nurse was a female *Shojo* (a submarine monster of dissipated habits). Even when my brother was a child he cried for *saké*. We see him at a great disadvantage, for I know he possesses many admirable qualities. May be fraternal affection blinds me, still I cannot help loving and admiring him. The other day, when he was sleeping in the kitchen like a dead man, I looked at him, and thought how sad it was he had fallen so low. While I was thus thinking, I noticed his left hand was clenched about the scabbard of his long sword and that he grasped the hilt with his right, showing him to be on his guard. When I advanced he immediately opened his eyes and partly drew his weapon, then recognizing me, rolled over and resumed his slumber. During that moment I observed the blade, unlike its dilapidated scabbard, was as brilliant as an icicle or a fragment of crystal ; therefore, believe, spite of his failing, Red-fence is not unmindful of the duties of a *samurai*, and I am certain we shall yet feel proud of him."

CHAPTER XXX.

'The years have come and gone, and I am still weeping for thee,
my beloved.
My tears fall day and night, like the waters of Nonobiki."

This poem admirably describes the grief of Lady
Pure-gem, who, on the third anniversary of her husband's death, had been all the day prostrated before
the family altar, where, with Lady Pine-island, she repeated prayers for the repose of the dead chieftain's
soul.

Toward the evening, when the storm was abating,
she yielded to the earnest solicitations of her faithful
attendant, and retiring to her private apartment, partook of some slight refreshment.

" Ah!" she exclaimed, gazing upon a *manrio*-plant
placed upon the *tokonoma*, " my dear husband wrote
his last poem in praise of yonder beautiful object.
That flourishes, while my beloved lord is no more ; his
family name has become extinct, his retainers are scat-

tered like the seeds of a thistle, and oh, terrible thought! his death remains unavenged."

" My honored mistress, do not despair," said Lady Pine-island. " Sir Big-rock will yet be heard from. The fire of loyalty is only slumbering in the hearts of our clansmen,"

The widow covered her face with her sleeves, and after sobbing awhile, said

" I hope your words will prove true. Remembering the nobility of my husband's character, his thoughtfulness for his retainers, his unbounded generosity, and the love they professed to bear for him, I cannot understand why they have permitted the leaves of three autumns to fall upon his tomb without having made an attempt to wipe out the disgrace of his death. Why has Big-rock not sent me some communication? I am living here secluded from the world, and ought to be informed of what the clansmen are doing."

Lady Pine-island did not reply, she having taken great care to prevent her mistress from hearing the strange rumors concerning Sir Big-rock.

About the hour of the Hog (8 P.M.), as Lady Pure-gem was returning to resume her prayers, a servant announced the arrival of Sir Big-rock.

In an instant the mourner's grief appeared to vanish, and she joyfully directed Lady Pine-island to conduct the visitor to her presence.

The attendant made her obeisance and retired, presently returning with the Chief-councillor, who was clad in his ceremonial robes. He advanced with a sorrowful face and grave demeanor, and kneeeling, prostrated himself before Lady Pure-gem, remaining with his forehead close to the mat, mute with grief.

Though the lady was likewise deeply moved, through her sadness came a gleam of joy, as she believed Sir Big-rock was there to announce the good news. When she had somewhat recovered from her emotion she requested Lady Pine-island to retire, then filled a cup with *saké* and offered it to her visitor, saying :

" I am told, after you left our castle you went to reside in Yamashina. What has brought you from so great a distance ? "

The councillor took the cup, and bowing, drained its contents, after which he replied :

" Most worthy-to-be-honored mistress, in the days of our dead lord's prosperity the responsibilities of my office gave me no time for relaxation, and during my brief visits to this city I had little opportunity for amusement. Although I am only a man of wave-like fortune, I, through the generosity of my honored chief, possess sufficient means for all my needs. You desire to know what has brought me from Yamashina ? It is this : Having exhausted all the delights of Kioto, I have visited Yedo to enjoy more fashionable pleasures."

The lady listened as though unwilling to credit her senses, seeing which, Sir Big-rock, who was secretly delighted with the success of his words, said :

"I have been to nearly all the celebrated places in this city, and only one more errand remains to be performed—that I shall accomplish to-night. My companions are notified and are waiting to accompany me. I have come to bid you a respectful farewell, as I may not return to Yedo for some years. Meanwhile may happiness and prosperity attend you."

Lady Pure-gem regarded him with amazement, utterly unable to understand the change in his sentiments. Her soul became filled with indignation, and losing her self-control, she exclaimed :

"Ingrate! Are you the loyal retainer of whom my dear lord said : 'Whatever may occur, I desire you will place implicit confidence in my Chief-councillor and regard his words as though they were mine?' Oh, unfaithful and miserable wretch, you have dishonored the name of *samurai*!"

In her agony and despair she grasped a paper-weight shaped like a horse, and hurled it at him.

Sir Big-rock caught the missile, and reverently pressing it to his forehead, replied :

"This parting gift of a horse,* I receive with profound thanks. Most worthy-to-be-honored, mistress, have you any message for your dead lord in heaven?"

Upon hearing this speech, Lady Pure-gem clasped her hands, and gazing earnestly at him, thought :

* "The horse is considered a lucky animal. Japanese history records many instances where a general, upon sending a warrior into a desperate combat, presented him with a steed, such a gift being regarded as a good omen."

" Can it be possible he is still loyal ? " then said, in a faltering voice :

" Sir Chief-councillor, I do not understand your meaning."

Sir Big-rock, recollecting how nearly he had betrayed himself, cautiously answered

" Honored Mistress, I regard your present as though it came from my dead chief. I beg you will now excuse me. Once more I bid you farewell."

He bowed respectfully to the floor, and rising, slowly retired from the apartment, leaving the lady bewildered and shocked at his inexplicable behavior.

The ante-chamber, to which Lady Pine-island had withdrawn, was merely a portion of the main room, shut off with paper screens so as to form a recess. Against the left wall stood an open press furnished with cupboards and drawers for garments ; it likewise contained a number of shelves filled with exquisite specimens of porcelain and old lacquer-ware. The chief attendant was reclining behind a paper-screen, her countenance betraying the indignation that possessed her soul. On her left were a pipe, and a lacquered. box holding a jar of finely shredded tobacco, and before her a tiny porcelain stove which supported a tea-pot. The other articles furnishing the place were a lacquered tray containing cups, a wooden pillow, a silken-wadded quilt, and a tall, square lantern, the sides of which were filled with semi-transparent paper.

Extending one of the volumes toward him, she exclaimed : " Sir Big-rock, we expected better things than this ! "

Chap. III, p. 217.

"Madam," said Sir Big-rock, sinking upon his knees and drawing some books from his left sleeve, "here are a few songs and poems I composed on my way from Kioto. In these volumes are described many places of beauty and historic fame. I believe their perusal will greatly interest our honored mistress ; therefore, beg you will present them to her and request she will honor me by reading them."

Although Lady Pine-island was intensely indignant with the speaker, she could not refuse the proffered gift, such a proceeding being contrary to etiquette. She took the volumes, opened one of them upside down, and extending it toward him, exclaimed :

" Sir Big-rock, we expected better things than this. It appears, instead of remembering your duty, you have thought no more of it than of a drop of dew, and have been amusing yourself and spending your time in verse-making. Pardon my plain speech. I cannot remain silent."

The other ladies of the household, who one by one had entered the apartment, united in expressing their contempt for his strange behavior ; however, Sir Big-rock merely bowed gravely, and taking his short sword from the floor, retired, followed by the young women, who accompanied him to the veranda, and continued their bitter reproaches as long as he remained in sight.

Lady Pine-island slipped the volumes into her sleeve,

deeming it would be an insult to present them to her mistress, after which she proceeded to the adjoining room where she found Lady Pure-gem prostrate before the altar, praying and sobbing as though she would die of grief.

CHAPTER XXXI.

Sir Big-rock quitted Lady Pure-gem's residence as the temple bells boomed forth the hour of the Fox (10 P.M.). The storm had ceased, and the full moon, shining through the cloud rifts, brilliantly illuminated the grounds surrounding the mansion. On reaching the shrine of the god-Fox, he paused, and gazing upon the snow-laden branches of the bamboos that overhung the structure, said :

" Thus have the loyal hearts of the clansmen been bowed with sorrow. To-morrow's sun will melt your burden and find us freed of a heavy load."

He moved on and passing the guard, who saluted him with profound respect, entered the street. After walking a few paces, he engaged a public *kago* and directed the bearers to convey him to his lodgings. The journey occupied nearly an hour, the distance from the Blue-hill district to the neighborhood of Sir Kira's mansion being over four miles. While proceeding by that noble's residence, they heard sounds

of music and revelry, and one of the coolies remarked
to the other :

" Sir Kira is giving a great feast ; we had better return here. It will be a good place for us to find another patron. We may earn a large sum between
this and mid-night."

When Sir Big-rock arrived at his destination, he detained his bearers until he had changed his robes of
ceremony for his armor and the uniform provided by
the contractor. After doing this he re-entered the
kago and was conveyed to the buckwheat-vermicelli
restaurant, where he was welcomed by his companions and the proprietor, who quickly set before them
an excellent repast.

" Gentlemen," said Mr. Long-time, producing a very
large and beautiful cup, " I was awarded this as the
champion's prize in a game of *hai-kai* (verse-making).
Will you empty it with me ? On the point of depart-
ing upon a journey, drinking from such a cup always
brings good luck."

Speaking thus, he placed the vessel before Sir Big-
rock.

The conspirators glanced significantly at one another, and were greatly delighted at his words. When
all had filled and emptied the cup, the Chief-councillor
said :

" Mr. host, we return you many thanks for offering
us the use of your treasure. Will you not confer another favor upon us, and recite the verse that won this
prize ? "

He took a brush and, leaning upon his sword, bent forward and wrote.

"It was nothing extraordinary," the man replied. "I gained the championship more by good luck than by the elegance of my stanzas. I fear you will deem it a very poor composition."

"Oh no! oh no!" they cried. "We are sure it is a most excellent poem. Please oblige us by reciting it."

"Well," he answered, "as you insist, I will comply. This is my poor attempt at versification:

> "During the night
> Sings high in the sky
> (What?) a nightingale."

"That is very good," exclaimed Sir Big-rock. "It may also be read thus:

> "In the world
> What will always attain eminence?
> (This) genius.

Your poem has set me verse-making. Please bring me writing materials. I will borrow your first stanza and add something to it."

He took a brush, and leaning upon his sword, bent forward and wrote:

> "During the night
> Harder grows
> (What?) the icicle."

Upon completing this he turned to Sir Big-eagle, and handing him the brush, remarked :

" Now see what you can do. We will have a verse-making match."

The *samurai* thought for a moment, and wrote :

" The cry of the sparrow-eagle pierces the sky."

To this Sir Hatchet added :

" Already the big *saké* cup has been emptied."

The last to write was Sir Big-rock, Jr., who composed the following :

" The red glow fills the hall of the Pine-trees."

These impromptu verses showed the spirit of their writers, and that, even in the presence of death, they were calm and resolute.

Among the party were some more proficient in warfare than in verse-making, who looked on respectfully, yet failed to comprehend the hidden meaning of the sentences.

Sir Unconquerable was of this number. After he had disposed of a good meal, he whispered to Sir Big-eagle

" Why does that poetry so greatly please our comrades ? For my part, I cannot see any sense in it."

His companion replied in a low voice :

"Listen. 'During the night harder grows the icicle,' may be read thus : 'During the night sharper grows the blade of the sword.' My verse also means : 'The sound of the whistle pierces the air.' Sir Hatchet's stanza signifies : 'Already Sir Kira has fallen,' and the poem of Sir Big-rock, Jr., may be interpreted in this manner : 'The red glow of the combat fills the hall decorated with the representations of Pine-trees,' the apartment in which Sir Kira has entertained his guests."

Sir Unconquerable's grim visage relaxed into a smile, and filling a cup with *saké* he drained it, then said :

" I understand, this is the hour of the poets ; later on I will try to distinguish myself. My poetry is written with the point of my sword."

While the conspirators were feasting, Sir Big-rock noticed the absence of Sir Shell, and conjecturing the cause, quietly called Sir Cedar-valley aside and whispered :

" Your friend, Sir Shell, has not yet arrived. I think it will be as well for you to seek him. In parting with wife and child, one forgets how the time flies."

Sir Cedar-valley retired from the assembly and hastened to the house of his friend, whom he found preparing to depart. Mrs. Home was weeping bitterly, and the child was clinging to her and lisping :

" Mamma, mamma, papa shall not go."

Sir Shell glanced at the visitor, as a condemned man does at his executioner, then turned from him, and folding his arms, endeavored to control himself.

" Comrade," said Sir Cedar-valley, crouching near him, " your companions are ready to start. I am certain you will not be the one to delay our journey."

For a moment Sir Shell remained mute and irresolute, after which, remembering his duty, he gazed sorrowfully at his beloved ones, and silently bidding them adieu, quitted his home, leaving his wife prostrate on the floor, like one struck down by lightning. The last sound he heard was the voice of little Also-five-boy, pitifully exclaiming :

" Papa! papa! "

When he joined his companions at the restaurant, he seated himself with a calm air and in no way betrayed the distraction of his soul.

Sir Big-rock did not appear to notice Sir Shell's entrance, which had been accomplished so quietly that few of the party knew he had not been with them all the evening.

Toward midnight the conspirators quitted the restaurant and proceeded across the Two-provinces Bridge. The cold was intense, and they did not encounter any one on their way.

Upon arriving at their rendezvous, a spot called Rush-island, they were joined by the second division from the tea-house.

Here they remained until the hour of the Ox
(2 A.M.), when they were formed into two companies;
the first under Sir Big-rock, and the second led by Sir
Big-rock, Jr., assisted by Sir Lucky-field. Each man
was clad in uniform, and carried in his sleeve a document describing the reason for the attack, to which
were affixed his names and a description of his per-
sonal appearance.

The following instructions, issued by Sir Big-rock,
were copied from the original document, preserved to
this day in the Spring-hill Temple :

1. Do not make any mistake in replying to signs
and signals. At the sound of the drum, beaten according to the code of Yamashika, nine times in three
turns, both the front and rear companies are simul-
taneously to advance.

2. Remember the watch-words—they are most
important, and have ever, during the night attacks of
all ages, been thus regarded.

3. To the challenge of " Mountain," give as a
counter-sign, " Spray," " Bubble," or any word referring to water.

4. To the challenge of " River," answer " Rock,"
" Valley " or " Top," or give a word referring to
mountain.

5. Reply as quickly and as clearly as possible, and
avoid combating with a friend.

6. As soon as we have gained an entrance to the

residence, search for the enemy's weapons, cut the strings of their bows, destroy the arrows, and break the spears.

7   Put out all lights and pour water into the fire-boxes ; the darkness will prevent our opponents from ascertaining our numbers, and the steam from the embers will greatly alarm them.   After that be ready to light your candles.

8.   Each man shall carry a bottle of alcohol for the purpose of dressing wounds and making flashes to dismay the foe.

9.   Each shall also carry two candles and two bamboo pins to be used for sticks.

10.   Before starting take some medicine.   Do this, no matter whether you be well or sick ; sudden excitement often makes a strong man ill.

11.   Do not fail to have your distinguishing letter, not only on your uniforms, but also upon your weapons and accoutrements.

12.   Each shall carry a *yatate* (pocket writing-case).

13.   After securing an entrance, bar all the doors and guard the places of exit.

14.   Each shall carry a blue silk wrapping cloth.

15.   When Sir Kira is found, his captors must blow three prolonged blasts upon their whistles, to which every one will respond, then all will assemble on the spot where he is discovered.

16.   Do not kill women or children, or any of the enemy who are unarmed.

At the moment when the leaguers were advancing upon the residence of Sir Kira, that noble, inflamed with his potations, was reclining upon his bed, thinking of the pleasures he had lately enjoyed, and never for an instant imagining that the hour of retribution was near.

CHAPTER XXXII.

SIR SMALL-GROVE.

" Good deeds are good seeds ;
Bad deeds are foul weeds."

In chapter eighth I related the story of the young merchant, Mr. Bright-stone, and his wife, Little-tiger I will now fulfil my promise, and describe how they were enabled to return the great kindness shown them by Sir Small-grove, Chief-councillor of Sir Kira.

It will be remembered that the young people were adopted by a mirror-maker. This good man died within a few months after he received them into his family, on hearing which Sir Small-grove advised Mr. Bright-stone to remove his place of business to a street adjoining the residence of Sir Kira.

On the night of the attack, Sir Small-grove, who had been all day in attendance upon his chief, was preparing to retire to bed, when he heard the sound of a drum followed by whistling and the crash of falling shutters. Comprehending in a moment the nature of the disturbance, he hastily awoke his little daughter,

228

Entering the house he hurriedly handed his daughter to the lady.

whom he loved very dearly. After cautioning the
child not to make any outcry, he took her in his arms,
and quitting his house, hurried across the enclosure to
a corner of the grounds where stood the temple of the
god of war, the rear eave of which overhung the street.
Sir Small-grove procured a fire-ladder, and ascending
to the roof, deposited his burden upon the snow-clad
slope, then drew up his means of escape and lowered
it on the other side of the wall. This accomplished,
he took the child upon his arm, rapidly descended to
the street, and started at a run toward the house of
Mr. Bright-stone, the inmates of which were fast
asleep, and who at first were greatly alarmed by his
summons. After a brief delay, during which they had
ascertained the name of their disturber, Mrs. Little-
tiger directed their boy-servant to withdraw the bolts
securing the entrance. When that was accomplished,
their visitor pushed aside the door, and entering "the
mouth of the house" hurriedly handed his daughter
to the lady, who anxiously enquired :

" What is the trouble, Sir Small-grove? Is your
dwelling on fire ? "

The *samurai* paused a moment, then replied :

" It is as I have often predicted. The calamity, so
long deferred, has at length overtaken my master.
The *yashiki* is invaded, and I have no expectation of
surviving the combat. For myself I care not ; my only
grief is on account of this dear child, who has already
lost her mother, and who, after my death, will have no
one to care for her. Remembering this I have

snatched a few moments of most precious time to bring her to you. My last wish is that you will bestow your kindness upon her."

He then rushed away without waiting to hear their assurance that " not even an ant should harm the little one."

Sir Small-grove remounted the useful ladder, and hastening to the mansion, threw himself into the thick of the fray, being particularly anxious to keep the leaguers from entering the sleeping apartment of Sir Kira before that noble had time to escape.

He guarded the door with indomitable bravery, and although desperately wounded, contrived to keep his assailants at bay, until, overpowered by numbers, he fell like a true *samurai*, and died in the act of defending his chief, his last effort being to hurl his sword at one of his opponents.

The whole mansion was a scene of confusion, and the cries of the women and children rose loud above the sounds of the combat. Barriers were forced, doors broken down, and the banqueting hall with its decorations of pine trees, crimsoned with the blood of both parties.

Outside, the bright stars twinkled in the clear sky, and the pale moon illuminated the snow-covered landscape.

When the conspirators entered Sir Kira's chamber, they discovered an empty bed. Though Sir Big-rock eagerly listened for the three blasts upon the whistle, no sound was heard but the clashing of weapons and the execrations of the combatants.

The whole mansion was a scene of confusion.

Chap. xxxii, p. 230.

CHAPTER XXXIII.

SIR BIG-ROCK'S GIFT.

" The long night is at an end.
   Brightly shines the sun of loyalty."

While the combat was raging in the mansion of Sir Kira, Lady Pine-island was seated by the fire-box on the floor of her apartment, thinking of Sir Big-rock.

Her companion was still in attendance upon their mistress and her own maid away visiting, so she felt lonely and disinclined to seek her bed. After smoking several pipes she took the books from her sleeve, and as the golden moments melted, sat musing with a heavy heart, her thoughts running thus

" The much trusted and long looked-for Sir Big-rock has been here, and the result is a bitter disappointment to us all. How different he is to what we have believed him to be ; how rude and stupid ! Why, he did not appear to understand the cause of our lady's just indignation, and after outraging her feelings, left these volumes for her. How strangely unreliable is the human heart! There is now no longer

231

any hope of avenging the wrongs of our house. Alas! how well I know it!"

The hours passed swiftly, and presently drowsiness overcame her loyal spirit; her fingers relaxed, the books slipped from her grasp and she slumbered. Then the sliding-door upon her right was gently pushed back and some one stealthily entered the apartment.

The noise, slight as it was, aroused the sleeper, who, fearing treachery, pretended to be unconscious, and with partly opened eyelids watched the intruder, a maid servant she had lately engaged, whom every one believed to be half witted.

The lady closely followed the other's movements, and soon discovered her object was to obtain possession of the volumes. As the thief stretched forth her hand, Lady Pine-island picked up a pipe and dealt her a sharp blow upon the knuckles. This did not stop the girl, who seized the books and endeavored to make off with them ; whereupon her mistress, who now began to comprehend the creature's treachery, grasped her by the robe and exclaimed

"We have been fools to imagine you were one. Ah! you are a spy sent by our enemy, Sir Kira. Wretch! I command you not to move another step."

The intruder finding herself and mission discovered, struggled violently to escape ; however, her captor held her firmly, crying :

"Help! help! There's an evil-doer in my chamber. In the name of our lady, I entreat for assistance."

There was a rush of persons from all parts of the house, and the girl was quickly secured and consigned to safe quarters.

When the ladies had retired and Pine-island somewhat recovered from her agitation, she took the books from the floor, and opening the first of them, began to peruse its contents. After reading a few pages, she placed her hands upright, palm to palm, and exclaimed:

"Spirits of my ancestors! what have I done? This very night Sir Kira is to be punished. The death of our dear lord and the dishonors heaped upon his house, have by this time been avenged. I now understand the motives of Sir Big-rock whom, alas! we treated so contemptuously. He feared that spies might have entered our household, therefore dared not even whisper the truth, believing, if he did so, the news might be conveyed to Sir Kira and thus put him on his guard. The Chief-councillor indeed came to bid us a long farewell. The act of that wretched girl proves the vigilance of our foe and the necessity for Sir Big-rock's caution. I must hasten to my lady and communicate this joyful intelligence."

She then hurriedly arranged her *obi* (girdle), and taking the volumes in her hand quitted the chamber. As she did so the crowing of the roosters announced the dawn of day.

Upon entering the corridor she beheld the ladies-in-waiting sitting in groups, and heard them commenting upon the events of the night.

" Be quick and prepare yourselves to attend upon your mistress," she cried. " You will shortly be required to receive important visitors." At these words they scattered to their apartments and were soon busy with combs, powder and paint.

The chief-attendant found Lady Pure-gem asleep, notwithstanding which she awoke her and related the welcome news.

" Pine-island," joyfully exclaimed the widow, "draw aside the window-screens."

When this was done they beheld the sun-goddess slowly arise from her bed among the purple clouds. The rays glinted across the snowy landscape and all nature appeared to rejoice, while the words written by the Chief-councillor, illuminated with happiness the soul of the Lady of Ako.

" The gods be praised!" she fervently ejaculated. " The spirit of my murdered husband will now rest in peace."

CHAPTER XXXIV

RETRIBUTION.

"In the day of his power his voice was loud and arrogant.
When justice overtook him he crouched mute and terrified."

It was the hour of the Tiger (4 A. M.); the combat
between the large body of well-disciplined warriors
who defended the residence of Sir Kira and the small
company of resolute leaguers was at an end, and the
aides of Sir Big-rock were searching the *yashiki* in
order to discover the fugitive noble, when Sir Straight-
grove and Sir Lull, Jr., entered a charcoal-house in the
rear of the mansion and began to probe the packages
with their spears. While they were thus engaged,
some one secreted behind a pillar hurled a bag of charcoal at Sir Straight-grove, then rushed at him furiously. At the same instant a second assailant con-
fronted Sir Lull, Jr.

The fight was brief, and the conspirators were the
victors.

"Come," said Sir Straight-grove, taking his dark lantern from his belt and flashing the light upon the scene, "where you find one snake it is as well to look for others. Those fellows did not attack us without good cause."

They minutely searched the building, which was half filled with bags of charcoal and billets of wood.

"What is that in yonder corner?" said Sir Straight-grove, advancing to the far end of the shed. "Is it a dog?

He stooped, and to his delight discovered the object was a man, dressed in a white satin sleeping-robe, blackened all over with charcoal.

Upon being addressed the fugitive refused to reply, finding which Sir Lull, Jr., dragged him out of the corner, and his comrade, turning the light upon the prisoner's face, exclaimed :

"It is Sir Kira! There is the scar upon his forehead!"

The overjoyed *ronin* gave the signal agreed upon, and the forty-five came hurrying to the spot.

Sir Big-rock directed the captors to bring their prisoner into the yard, then proceeded to ascertain the truth of the announcement ; meanwhile his followers gathered round and silently awaited the result of his investigation. After looking intently at the blackened features of the man, he said :

"Yes, this is Sir Kira."

He knelt before the trembling noble, and addressing him respectfully, said :

"Sir Kira, we are the retainers of Lord Morning-field, who, at your instigation, was condemned to *hara-kiri.* We have come hither to avenge him, and thus perform our duty as faithful, loyal men. We pray you will acknowledge the justice of our purpose, and beseech you to perform upon yourself the honorable ceremony. I will have the honor to act as your second."

Sir Kira glanced furtively at the assembled conspirators but stubbornly refused to reply, whereupon Sir Big-rock, finding it was useless to persuade him to die the death of a noble, produced the dirk of his dead lord, and handing it to Sir Lull, Jr., directed him to make use of it.

*   *   *   *   *   *   *

When the day broke the victorious leaguers quitted the *yashiki,* and forming into companies, proceeded across the Two-provinces Bridge toward the Spring-hill Temple.

After marching a short distance, Sir Big-rock ordered a halt, and summoning Temple-cliff, bade him communicate the news to Lady Pure-gem.

CHAPTER XXXV

THE COMMENTS OF THE CROWD.

"I listened to the voices of the people and heard of the noble
deed done in the night."

The morning of the 15th of December dawned clear
and bright, and the household of Sir Turf-ground slumbered peacefully. To the family of a *samurai* one day
is like another, and there is no difference between
the first month and the last; to the merchant, the
settling of accounts causes December to be a busy
time.

It was nearly the hour of the Dragon (8 A.M.) when
Sir Turf-ground, who was still in bed, heard the sound
of many persons passing his window, and voices in
loud conversation.

"Look! there they go along that street," cried one.
"Come quickly."

"Here, Good-fellow, I must leave you and hurry
on by myself. You move more like a tortoise than a
man. We shall not get a glimpse of them."

"Wait a moment. Confound it! You surely will

not go without me. I was the one to tell you the news."

" Look ! Look ! they are coming this way," cried a woman. " Hurry, my son, or we shall miss them."

Then came a noise of persons moving over the frozen snow, and a dull roar, such as is made by a crowd when admiring a procession.

At first Sir Turf-ground did not pay much attention, but when he heard the people murmuring their applause, he hurriedly arose, dressed himself, thrust his swords into his belt, and opening the window, beheld the people running toward the end of the street. He called to his wife and while he was interrogating her, one of the spectators shouted to him, saying

" Have you seen them ? By the gods, it is a glorious spectacle ! "

" What is ? " demanded Sir Turf-ground. " Tell me the news."

" The *ronin* of Ako have attacked the residence of Sir Kira and taken his head. They are now on their way to deposit it upon the tomb of their lord."

As the man was speaking, a store-keeper came rushing up the street, crying :

" They have just entered the *yashiki* of the Lord of Sendai. Be quick if you wish to see them. It was a sight to behold the brave ones forcing their way in regular order and guarding themselves according to the rules of war. Ah! they are loyal and faithful men ! "

Sir Turf-ground listened attentively, his first thought being of his brother, and he whispered to his wife :

" I am certain Red-fence is one of that party."

He went out into the veranda where he found his old servant, who was on his knees playing with a pair of puppies, and whom he thus addressed :

" First-fellow, do you know the truth about this great excitement ? "

" Yes, my master. Upon hearing the noise I and many persons quitted the *yashiki* and entered the street in order to investigate the matter. The *ronin* of Ako have performed their duty and are now returning. I am sure Sir Red-fence is with them."

" I know not what to think," said Sir Turf-ground. " The other *ronin* being the hereditary retainers of the Lord of Ako, might be willing to avenge their master's wrongs, but my brother was only affiliated to the clan, added to which he is generally under the influence of *saké*, and would, I fear, be unable to take part in such a glorious deed. Yet there is a strange coincidence between his message to me last night and the rumor of this morning. I agree with you in believing he is with them. If this is so, it will be not only a great honor to him, but also to me."

" Honorable master, shall I run out and ascertain ? "

" Stay one moment, First-fellow. If I send you on such an errand and my brother is not among the noble band, I shall become a laughing-stock. You had better go out as though by accident. Having ascertained the truth, come back quickly."

"First-fellow, do you know the truth about this great excitement?"

Chap. xxxv. p. 20.

" Very well, honorable master, I will return as soon as possible and ease your mind."

He ran to the kitchen and procured a basket and account-book, as if he were going to market, then went by the side-gate and pushed through the dense .ass of people.

After the servant was gone, Sir Turf-ground paced the veranda and prayed to the gods that his brother might be found among the loyal men.

First-fellow moved in and out between the spectators congregated upon the avenue leading to the residence to the Lord of Sendai, and kept his ears open for news.

Presently a tall man, in the front rank of the crowd, looked back and said :

" No one will be able to go any further. The watchmen of the Lord of Sendai have formed a line across the street in front of the residence and made a fence with their clubs."

" *Oi*, Silver-boy ! " cried a broad-shouldered fellow, " have you seen them ? "

" Yes, I caught a glimpse of the party as they entered the gate. They must have fought bravely, for their armor was cut all to pieces, and many of them were desperately wounded."

Then a number of persons spoke at once, saying :

" Are they going to stay inside ? "

" I hope they will soon come out."

" What gallant men ! "

"This is just what we expected of the *ronin* of Ako."
Every one was enthusiastic over the courage and
loyalty of the forty-seven, and adding rumor to rumor
in the exaggerated fashion of a crowd, they wore the
time away.

" Pine-boy," exclaimed a young clerk, " where have
you been ? You look as though you had spent the
night in emptying a jar."

The man addressed, who was nodding as though
half asleep, opened his eyes and replied :

" Ah! Seven-fields, my boy, is that you? You
have, as usual, missed a great sight by not going with
me."

"I do not miss your headache," retorted Seven-fields.

" You are mistaken," answered the drowsy man.
" I drank very little *saké ;* the fact is, I spent the night
at the residence of my cousin, Plum-garden, who lives
near the *yashiki* of Sir Kira. As we were retiring to
bed, we heard the sound of the drum and the crash of
the attack, whereupon we ascended to the roof of the
house, which overlooked the grounds of the noble's
mansion. By the gods! it was a tremendous fight.
The armies on both sides, with their banners flying,
fought in four directions, the war-cry sounding from
the earth to the heavens, and for awhile it seemed as
if the mighty mountains would be rent asunder.
Presently, from the attacking army, issued a warrior
on horseback, clad in purple armor, with a coat of red
and white "——

" One moment," cried Seven-fields.   " What are you romancing about ? "

" I am relating what I heard at the lecture in New Street the other night," replied the joker.   " Why don't you attend there and illuminate your mind? "

The young men laughed, and one of them remarked

" Pine-boy, you are always telling stories ; why do you not sometimes speak the truth ? "

The merry fellow made a grimace, and glancing round him, answered :

" Because fiction is considered more interesting than history.   *Oi*, you in the front rank, do you see anything of the second party of the *ronins ?* "

The people craned their necks, and Seven-fields eagerly exclaimed :

" Is there a second party?   I thought all the leaguers had entered the mansion of the Lord of Sendai."

" Oh! you are quite behind the times," laughingly remarked Pine-boy.   " The second company is far more numerous than the first.   It is composed of the ghosts of Sir Kira's men."

As he spoke there was a movement among the watchmen who guarded the entrance to the *yashiki*, and soon the cry went up :

" See, they are coming out ! "

" Yes, yes, here they are."

The people crowded forward, and the noise of their tongues was like the roar of advancing waters.

CHAPTER XXXVI.

SIR RED-FENCE WINS GOLDEN OPINIONS.

" The crooked tree often produces fine fruit.
A sword forged by Masamune is sometimes found in a second-hand store."

The *ronin* had been entertained by the Lord of Sendai, who, on hearing of their approach, had sent a messenger inviting them to enter his mansion and partake of refreshments ; his action showing to the world his thorough approval of their deed.

Upon quitting his residence they formed into three companies, and with their arms ready for use, marched boldly forward.

First-fellow elbowed his way into the front rank of the crowd, and eagerly waited for the approach of the companies.

The vanguard, led by Sir Unconquerable, whose armor hung about him like the rags of a beggar, went by, but though First-fellow closely scanned their faces he failed to see the object of his search.

Then came the second division, under Sir Big-rock.

This company, the largest, was almost entirely composed of wounded men, many of whom were carried in *kago* (litters). As these passed, the crowd commented upon the fact, that while a great number of the defenders of Sir Kira were killed, not one of the *ronin* had fallen in the attack.

First-fellow, who began to feel very nervous, anxiously watched for the arrival of the third company. As they came in sight his apprehension vanished, for, marching at the head, he beheld Sir Red-fence, who, instead of walking with his usual unsteady gait, advanced with a firm step and a martial bearing that elicited the admiration of the beholders. His head was bare, his helmet being pushed back and suspended from his neck by its cord; his brow was bound with a white ribbon, and in his hand he carried a spear.

He soon perceived his brother's servant, whom he beckoned to him and thus addressed :

" I am glad to see you, First-fellow."

The man went upon his knees in the snow, and bowing his head to the ground, said :

" Sir Red-fence, I offer you my hearty congratulations. You look very weary."

" If I do, I am not sensible of any such feeling," was the reply. " Last night I went to bid my brother farewell, and was unfortunate enough to miss seeing him, and, to add to my regret, my sister was indisposed and unable to receive me. After leaving them, I, with others, paid a visit to Sir Kira whom we found at home."

While the *ronin* was addressing First-fellow, the latter rubbed his hands together and chuckled to himself as though delighted at beholding such a change in his employer's relative, and when the latter ceased speaking, he replied :

" This morning as soon as my honorable master was told of the attack, he ordered me to run with all speed and ascertain whether you were among the noble band. When he learns the good news his heart will leap with joy. I am delighted to be the bearer of such glorious tidings."

Sir Red-fence laughed heartily and said :

" The fact was my brother rather doubted my presence here? Come now, First-fellow, acknowledge the truth."

" Honorable sir, you are indeed mistaken. The moment we heard what had occurred, my master and mistress, myself and all our people, immediately said : 'Sir Red-fence is one of the loyal men,' and I rushed off to ascertain whether you were wounded, and to learn from your own lips the particulars of the victory."

The *ronin* smiled significantly and handed his whistle and spear-badge to the man, saying :

" Present these, my last gifts, to my honored brother. Tell him that we have avenged our master's death and, bearing the evidence on our bodies, are proceeding to his tomb at the Spring-hill Temple, where we hope to join our honored lord. I send both my brother and his wife a parting prayer for their happiness." He

"Present these, my last gifts, to my brother."

Chap. xxxvi. p. 246.

next removed his purse from his girdle and presenting it to the kneeling man, said in a kindly voice: " This is for you. Now, First-fellow, I must hurry away or I shall be left behind. Take care of yourself and be diligent in the performance of your duties."

Uttering these words he turned and hastened after his comrades who were already at some distance.

For a few moments First-fellow was unable to suppress his joy; meanwhile the crowd collected about him and began to ask questions.

" Look at him!" he cried, as though the *samurai* were still present. " Honorable sirs, that is Sir Red-fence, the brother of my honorable master. He was adopted into the family of Red-fence of the clan of Ako and is one of the party of avengers."

" Why, old fellow," remarked a tanner among the spectators, " what are you talking about ? The gentleman you are praising is out of sight."

" Ha! Ha! Ha!" laughed the bystanders. " He is crazy with joy."

These remarks brought First-fellow to his senses, and springing to his feet he ran with all his speed toward the residence of his employer, whom he found anxiously awaiting his arrival.

First-fellow fell upon his knees and, panting, exclaimed :

" Honorable master, I could not return a moment sooner."

Sir Turf-ground's heart beat so quickly that he was

unable to reply in his usual voice, and could only whisper :

"Have you seen my brother? Not a shadow of him, I suppose?"

"You are wrong, honorable master. Be happy, he was there. I found the avenues crowded with people. *Samurai*, merchants, old and young, men, women and children, were mingled together without any distinction. I pushed my way through them and, as I neared the residence of the Lord of Sendai, beheld the loyal men emerging from the gateway. There were some fifty of them, and though nearly all were wounded, they offered a bold front and advanced in battle array. It was a stirring sight."

"Wounded did you say?" anxiously enquired Sir Turf-ground. "How is it with my brother?"

"He is uninjured," replied the servant; then, sitting up, he slapped his hands on his knees and exclaimed : "Ah! he is a brave man. As he marched at the head of the third company every one applauded him. Instead of the shabby swords to which our eyes have been so long accustomed, he wore beautiful weapons, the scabbards of which were inlaid with gold and silver, and his spear bore ample evidence of having been used. When he called 'First-fellow' I was so overcome that my heart ceased to beat."

"My thanks to the gods," said Sir Turf-ground. "How bright has the world become to me!"

The servant took the whistle and badge from

his bosom and as he handed them to his master, said :

" Sir Red-fence sent these to you and bade me re-peat this message : ' Brother, I am on the road to death, receive these trifles as my parting gift.' To me he gave this purse of money. Oh! how we have misunderstood him! He is a most loyal, noble man."

First-fellow burst into tears, overcome with the rec-ollection of the scene through which he had just passed.

Sir Turf-ground, no longer able to repress his emo-tion, wept with joy, feeling happy beyond measure that his brother should have so nobly fulfilled the first duty of a *samurai*, and conferred honor upon the house of his ancestors.

He dismissed his servant with warm words of ap-proval, and hastened in-doors where he received the congratulations of his wife and the maids. The latter fully appreciated the gallant conduct of their master's relative and were loud in their praises of the once despised Red-fence.

The news soon spread through the *yashiki*, and the house of Sir Turf-ground was crowded with the clans-men of Autumn-moon, who complimented him upon the loyalty of his brother, all agreeing that it was not only an honor to the clan of Ako but also to their own. In their enthusiasm each begged for some memento of Sir Red-fence, and hearing of the bottle, asked for a few drops of the *saké*, with which they bathed the crowns of their heads. Having done this they put on the old rain-hat and prayed that the spirit of its owner might inspire them to follow his example.

Sir Turf-ground, who regarded the earthen vessel as a precious relic, wrapped it in a piece of purple silk and placed it in a box among his treasures.

This souvenir is said to be preserved by his descendants, even to the present day, and is the foundation of the well-known story of " Red-fence and his *saké* bottle."

CHAPTER XXXVII.

SUMMONING THE WITNESS.

" Though the sun is shining, and the snow has melted from the face of nature, our sleeves are moistened with tears."

While the *ronin* were being entertained by the Lord of Sendai, the messenger despatched by Sir Big-rock arrived at the residence of Lady Pure-gem and requested permission to see the mistress.

As soon as his arrival was announced, Lady Pine-island entered the reception hall, and saluting him, said :

" I should imagine by your appearance that you are the messenger we have been so anxiously expecting. Surely I remember your face. Are you not the loyal soldier, Temple-cliff?"

He bowed and replied :

" That is my humble name. I come from the Chief-councillor to bring you joyful news."

" Follow me," she said ; " my lady must receive the information from your lips."

She conducted him to the presence of her mistress
and announced him, saying :

" This is Temple-cliff, who comes from Sir Big-
rock."

Lady Pure-gem glanced at his torn garments and
battered armor, which explained more eloquently than
words the desperate nature of the attack, and felt that
even this humble soldier had done his duty to her
beloved husband.

Temple-cliff prostrated himself at the entrance of
the apartment, and after saluting her, proceeded in a
rough, yet graphic fashion to relate the events of the
night.   His words, though homely, were full of eloquence, and deeply moved the hearts of the listeners.

As he spoke the tears streamed down his cheeks,
and at the conclusion of his recital he bowed his head
to the mat and remained exhausted with his effort.

Lady Pure-gem, after directing one of her attendants to give Temple-cliff a cup of *saké*, ordered him to
be conducted to a room where he received proper
attention and nourishment.

At the hour of the Horse (noon), a number of persons applied for entrance at the outer gate, and upon
being granted admittance, proved to be Sir Arrow-
head and one Temple-west, a servant of Sir Big-rock.
They were accompanied by six footmen and twenty
coolies, who bore the following packages :

Three locked trunks covered with oil paper.

A wooden box labeled " Books."

" Your Ladyship, I come from the Chief-councillor."

A small box containing a letter.

Nine thousand *rio* wrapped in paper.

Lady Pine-island directed the party to be conducted into the garden opposite the room in which her mistress was seated.

When the messengers saw Lady Pure-gem, they knelt and bowed their faces to the ground, after which the coolies and foot-servants advanced, placed their burdens upon the veranda and retired out of sight, leaving Sir Arrow-head who still remained in a respectful position.

"What is the meaning of this?" demanded Lady Pure-gem. "Arrow-head, come into the house and explain your mission."

The *samurai* rose, stepped upon the veranda, and prostrating himself, said :

"Your Lady-ship, I come from the Chief-councillor who is now with the loyal clansmen at the tomb of our honored lord. Sir Big-rock desires me to say this to your Lady-ship. 'At the surrender of the castle, I, as Chief-councillor, removed a large sum of money which I had the right to take. I have expended a portion of the amount for the support of certain members of the clan and for the armor and weapons required in carrying out our duty. There are nine thousand *rio* remaining which I beg your Lady-ship will accept. I also forward an account of my disbursements.'"

Lady Pure-gem was profoundly moved by this

speech, which not only proved the bravery and loyalty of the Chief-councillor, but showed he was anxious to provide for her future comfort.

" My honored and beloved husband spoke most truly," she exclaimed. " Big-rock is a man of a hundred thousand, brave, honorable, fertile in resource, patient under difficulties, and a thorough statesman. Can any one excel him ? "

She then whispered to Lady Pine-island and retired greatly agitated.

The chief attendant ordered the servants to see to the messengers, and when this was done they were conducted to the apartment of their mistress, who feasted them with many dainties and rewarded them with expressions of approval.

During the meal she made minute enquiries concerning each of the *ronin*, and, as she listened to the sad stories, wept over their sufferings and privations.

When the messengers were dismissed, Temple-cliff, who was the bearer of a letter from Sir Big-rock to his wife, set out for his destination, and Sir Arrow-head departed for the Spring-hill Temple. As the *samurai* quitted the residence, he encountered a third messenger, Sir Three-village, who, hastily saluting him, entered the house and asked permission to see their mistress.

Lady Pure-gem immediately agreed to grant him an interview.

On being admitted into her presence, he bowed profoundly, and raising his head, thus addressed her :

"Honorable mistress, I am charged to deliver this message. 'We, the loyal men, having betaken ourselves to the tomb of our late lord and expecting soon to be in the hands of the authorities, beg that some one be at once despatched from the household of your Lady-ship to witness the offering we are about to make to the spirit of our honored chief.'"

The lady reflected for a moment, then said to her chief-attendant:

"Pine-island, will you proceed with all despatch to the Spring-hill Temple and in my name thank each of the loyal retainers for his devotion to my never-to-be-forgotten lord. At the same time you will ask Big-rock to forgive me for ever having mistrusted him."

Lady Pine-island bowed and replied:

"I am conscious of my inability to perform so sacred and important an errand, yet to this and all your commands I joyfully assent."

She then dressed herself in her ceremonial robes and, entering a *norimono* (litter), was borne swiftly from the Western Hill to the region of the Eastern Sea.

Sir Three-village followed her, and when they arrived at the Spring-hill Temple, announced to the Chief-councillor

"Comrade, the witness deputed by our lady is in the waiting-room."

Sir Big-rock bowed and replied:

"Conduct her hither. We will now proceed with the ceremony."

CHAPTER XXXVIII.

"I knelt before the tomb of my chief and reverently addressed his noble spirit."

The afternoon sun, descending to its resting-place behind the hills, feebly struggled through the leafless branches of the trees that surrounded the little cemetery of the Spring-hill Temple. In the centre of the enclosure was the tomb of Lord Morning-field, consisting of three tiers of stone, surmounted by a massive, upright slab, which bore the *mon* (crest) of the house of Ako and the posthumous name of the *Daimio*.

" *Reiko in den Mayeno Shosho*
Chosantayu Suimo Genri Daikoji."

[Great-peacefully-reclining-*samurai* of the Cold-shining mansion, who, blowing aside a hair, revealed the hidden spirit of loyalty in his retainers ; and who, during his life, enjoyed the honorable title of Major-General and The-great-man-having-the-privilege-of-audience-with-the-Mikado-(Emperor).]

The tomb was enclosed with a stone railing and

256

surrounded by a platform of the same imperishable material, the slabs before the entrance being depressed a few inches so as to form a pathway.

Upon the second step rested a *mizuhachi* (stone trough for water), on each side of which were stone vases containing evergreens, among the latter being branches of the beautiful *manrio*.

Maku (cloth screens used for the purpose of enclosing a camp) had been erected around the edge of the platform, and the spot thus shut off from the gaze of the spectators who swarmed about the approaches to the cemetery.

As the bell of the temple slowly announced the hour of the Ape (4 P. M.), Lady Pine-island was conducted inside the enclosure and assigned a place, after which the *ronin*, who were resting in various attitudes, rose to the respectful position, and Sir Big-rock, addressing Sir Lull, Jr., said :

" Comrade, present our offering."

The *samurai* removed the cloth which covered an object resting upon a white-pine *sambo*, and raising the burden, slowly advanced inside the railings and deposited it upon the third step, then retired backward. As he did so a priest approached the tomb and set a lacquered *Dai* (stand) upon the flag-stone. On the stand was a bronze urn containing live charcoal, and a large jar filled with grains of incense.

The *ronin* then took their positions on the platform, Sir Big-rock kneeling nearest to the tomb on the left, and the others forming a semi-circle, his son occupying the second post of honor on the right.

The scene was most solemn and impressive, and Lady Pine-island bowed her head in her sleeves and wept audibly.

Sir Big-rock, whose face was pale with suppressed excitement, rose, and advancing to the incense stand, prostrated himself, remaining several moments with his forehead close to the stone.   Outside all was hushed, and no sound could be heard save the sobs of Lady Pine-island.

After a long pause the Chief-councillor took a scroll from his bosom and read as follows :

"December 15, 1701.

" We have this day come to do homage at your tomb, all of us being most willing to lay down our lives in your cause.   Spirit of our dead Lord, we reverently announce this to you.   Three years ago, you, our honored and beloved master, were pleased to attack Sir Kira, for what reason we know not.   You, our honored and beloved Lord, were compelled to put an end to your life, but Sir Kira was permitted to live. Although we fear after you have submitted to the decree, you will be displeased at our having resisted it, still we could not refrain from doing our duty.   We have eaten your food and partaken of your bounty ; we are yours in all things and have ever remembered the command of Confucius.   We would not dare to present ourselves before you in paradise without having carried out the vengeance you began. ' Every day we have waited has appeared like three autumns', yet, notwithstanding our loyal desire, three autumns have come and gone since we received your legacy. Verily ' we have trodden the snow for one day, nay, for two days, and have tasted food but once.' The old, feeble and sick, the young and strong, have come here joyfully to end their lives. Although men laughed at us as at the sickle-insect, which, trusting in the strength of its puny weapon, will attack a team of horses and bring itself to grief, we have never halted in our duty. Your enemy has hidden himself like a bat, and we have had great difficulty in finding him at home. Last night we called at his residence, and this day have escorted him to your tomb."

The Chief-councillor paused in his reading, and producing the dirk from his bosom, rose, advanced to the *sambo* and deposited the weapon by the offering ; then returned, knelt behind the incense-stand and resumed:

" This dirk, which you, our honored and beloved Lord, used upon your enemy and employed to sever the thread of your existence, and which, in your last hour, you solemnly committed to our charge, we now return. If your noble spirit be present, we entreat you, as a token, to once more grasp your weapon, and, a second time, strike the head of your foeman and thus forever end your feud.

" This is the prayer of your forty-seven humble retainers."

Sir Big-rock placed the document upon the tomb and all present prostrated themselves.

After a moment that seemed like an age, they felt the massive structure shaken as though by an earthquake, then came the sound of a dull thud, resembling the stroke of a dirk, and the weapon dropped from its place and fell near the right hand of Sir Big-rock, who reverently received the gift, and raising it to his forehead, cried :

" Master, we thank thee ! Now, come what may, we fear not, for you have approved of our deed. O noble spirit ! wait a little longer and you shall be once more surrounded by your loyal retainers."

The *ronin* listened to this speech with awed faces, then bowed to the ground and wept tears of joy.

When they became somewhat composed, the Chief-councillor took a few grains of incense from the vessel, and throwing them upon the burning embers, exclaimed :

" As this sweet perfume ascends from this vase, so will my soul soon leave its worthless body and join thee, my honored and beloved Lord, in the land of shadows."

He returned to his seat, and taking the roll-call, opened it and said in a firm voice :

" Big-rock, Jr."

His son bowed, and addressing his parent, said :

" Sir Chief-councillor, there are others who should precede me in this solemn act. Sir Straight-grove,

Sir Lull, Jr., Sir Common, Sir Hatchet, Sir Unconquerable, Sir Cliff-side, Sir Thousand-cliffs, Sir Island-in-the-front, Sir Red-fence, Sir Shell,—nay all should precede me. I, being the junior, ought to be the last to make my respectful offering."

The *ronin* admired the humility of their young comrade, and murmured approvingly ; then Sir Big-rock said :

" Your words fill me with happiness ; Sir Straight-grove and Sir Lull, Jr., shall precede you."

Sir Straight-grove advanced and performed the solemn rite, then bowing a second time, prayed for the repose of his mother's soul.

Sir Lull, Jr., took a large pinch of incense, the smoke of which was wafted like a dark cloud toward the offering on the *sambo.*

As Sir Big-rock, Jr., returned to his place he beheld, above the canvas screen surrounding the tomb, the peak of Fuji-yama, and remembering his wish, smiled and saluted it.

Sir Lucky-field, an old man who followed him, on resuming his seat, thought :

" The sun of to-day has dispelled the heavy snow of yesterday. The act I have just performed has relieved my soul of a grievous burden."

Next came Sir Lucky-field, Jr., who, like his father, felt at peace with all the world, and made his offering with a heart full of gratitude.

This young man was succeeded by Sir Common.

As the latter shook the incense upon the coals, big
tears trickled down his cheeks, for he remembered the
heroic deed performed by his mother.

Following him came Sir Hatchet who was, as usual,
calm and dignified. After he had performed the rite,
he seated himself next to Sir Common, and bowing
his head, thought

"The approval of our Lord fills our hearts with happiness, the reflection of which will render joyful those
who are dear to us."

While he was thinking, his adopted son, Sir Hatchet,
Jr., made his offering.

Then came Sir Moat, Sr., a very old man, who had
been desperately wounded in the attack, and who was
supported by his son, Sir Moat, Jr. The patriarch
spilt some of the incense, noticing which he said :

"That is a good omen; I shall not die of my wounds,
but shall end my life like the rest of my comrades."

After father and son had returned to their places,
Sir Lull, Sr., feebly rose, and motioning his sons to remain seated, crawled toward the incense stand, drag-
ging his left limb, which bore a frightful wound. Notwithstanding his injuries, he made his offering in a
resolute manner and spoke in a voice audible to those
outside the enclosure.

This brave man was followed by his second son,
who, having performed the loyal rite, returned to his
parent, when the latter said :

"My only regret is I have not forty-seven sons to
join in this joyful ceremony.'

He was succeeded by Sir Shoal, Sir Shoal, Jr., Sir Inner-field and Sir Inner-field, Jr., who burnt incense and addressed the spirit of their dead Lord.

" Sir Shell!" called the Chief-councillor.

The young *ronin*, who had sacrificed so much, advanced with a firm step, and being unable to use his right arm, made his offering with his left. He bowed silently and invoked the spirit of his chief, saying :

" O, beloved master ! I pray you remember my helpless wife and child!"

As he rose, Sir Cliff-side prepared to take his place. He, too, thought of his family, but remembering the words of his wife and the benevolent act of the god-Fox felt comforted.

This noble *samurai* was followed by Sir Tide-field and Sir Rich-grove, who, being severely wounded, were carried by their comrades, Sir Arrow-head and Sir Swift-water. These assisted the maimed men to make their offerings.

Sir Pure then advanced, and having performed the rite, resumed his seat, thinking :

" I shall soon make my last journey. This time I shall not require *kago*" (alluding to his quick and pain-ful trip from Yedo to Ako).

Sir Red-fence next responded to his name and reverently followed the example of his comrades. As he resumed his seat, he produced a bottle and cup, and addressing the Chief-councillor, said in a low voice :

"Having accomplished the duty required, I will now empty a cup of congratulation."

Sir Big-rock did not reply, knowing full well it would be easier to check a mountain torrent than to prevent *sake* from descending his comrade's throat.

Sir Tree-village, Sir Rush-valley, Sir Near-pine, Sir Thousand-horses, Sir Cedar-field, Sir Cliff-island and Sir Middle-village then answered to the summons, five of them being too badly crippled to burn the incense without help.

"Sir Unconquerable!"

The *ronin* rose slowly, as he did so the remnants of his armor fell upon the pavement, noticing which he kicked them aside and advanced to the stand.

This *samurai* took a handful of incense, and while it was being consumed, grimly watched the object on the *sambo.* He then offered a brief prayer ; as he resumed his place he said to Sir Hatchet

"The falling of the fragments of my armor, and my ragged condition, reminded me of the time when you called my name from the portal of the castle, though then my heart was heavily burdened, while now it is, like my body, free from encumbrances."

After him came Sir Village-pine, Sr., Sir Store-bridge, Sir Village-pine, Jr., Sir Faithful-friend, Sir Rush-field, Sir Arrow-field, Sir Victory-field, Sir Cliff-field, Sir Cross-river and Sir Three-village. These men being among the wounded, though not completely disabled, assisted one another.

When they had retired, Sir Island-in-the-front, Sir Thousand-cliffs and Sir Big-eagle, made their offerings. The Chief-councillor then said in a loud voice ; "Temple-cliff!" adding : " In the absence of our brave comrade, I will perform the rite for him."

Sir Big-rock burnt the incense, having done which he sent to the chief-priest, who, with his assistants, entered the enclosure, and advancing before the tomb, offered prayers, to which the *ronin* listened respectfully.

At the conclusion of the ceremonies, the Chief-councillor bowed to the *Sojo* (superior of the priests) and said :

" Will your reverence be good enough to take charge of our offering and have it disposed of according to the usual custom ? "

The *Sojo* gravely returned his salute and replied " Sir Big-rock, it is our duty to attend to the dead."

After the priests had retired, Lady Pine-island completed her errand, and, in the name of her mistress, thanked the loyal men for their devotion to their late lord ; then addressing the Chief-councillor, commenced the message she was charged to deliver, on hearing which he politely interrupted her, saying

" Pardon me, I only carried out the last wishes of my honored and beloved chief. My honored mistress thinks too much of the poor services I have been able to render her." He bade the lady a respectful farewell, remarking : "You were indeed fortunate to be present when the spirit of our honored chief gave its approval to the act we have performed. May you always be happy and enjoy good health."

As he finished speaking, one of the priests approached him and said :

"Sir Big-rock, the officers of the Sho-gun are in the reception hall and desire your attendance."

*   *   *   *   *   *   *

At the hour of the Hog (8 P. M.) a procession left the grounds of the Spring-hill Temple. First came a number of armed retainers carrying lanterns, decorated with the *mon* (crest) of Lord Narrow-river, Prince of Higo, who guarded a body of the *ronin*, including Sir Big-rock. Next a second detachment, consisting of *samurai* in the service of Lord Pine-plain, escorting twelve of the *ronin*, Sir Big-rock, Jr., being among the number. Following these marched the retainers of Lord Mori, who were in charge of the third division of prisoners ; then came a party of *ronin* who were in the custody of *samurai* belonging to the house of Lord Water-field.

They moved silently and proceeded slowly, in order that the coolies bearing the litters which contained the wounded, might not increase the sufferings of the loyal men.

Upon reaching the heart of the city the procession separated, and the officers in charge conveyed their prisoners to the *yashiki* of their respective lords.

From that time, pending the decision of the authorities, the *ronin*, though treated with the greatest consideration, were neither permitted to receive visits from their friends nor communicate with them. They were, in fact, dead to the world.

CHAPTER XXXIX.

THE RONINS REJOIN THEIR LORD.

" Fully conscious of having performed my duty, I joyfully salute
the messenger of death."

The authorities, having imprisoned the *ronin*, were
exceedingly perplexed how to act, their sympathy being entirely with the loyal band.

Early on the morning of the 4th of February, 1702,
Lord Narrow-river entered the hall in which Sir Big-
rock and his companions were confined, and after en-
quiring concerning their condition, said :

" It appears to me you must feel very weary of this
sort of existence ; however, be the news good or bad,
I imagine you will soon hear from the Council. Although you are not permitted to receive favors from
your friends, still there is no law to prevent me from
endeavoring to serve you after your sentence is
passed. Can I, in any way, show my appreciation of
your loyalty ? "

Sir Big-rock gravely saluted him, and replied :

" My Lord, in the name of my comrades, I thank

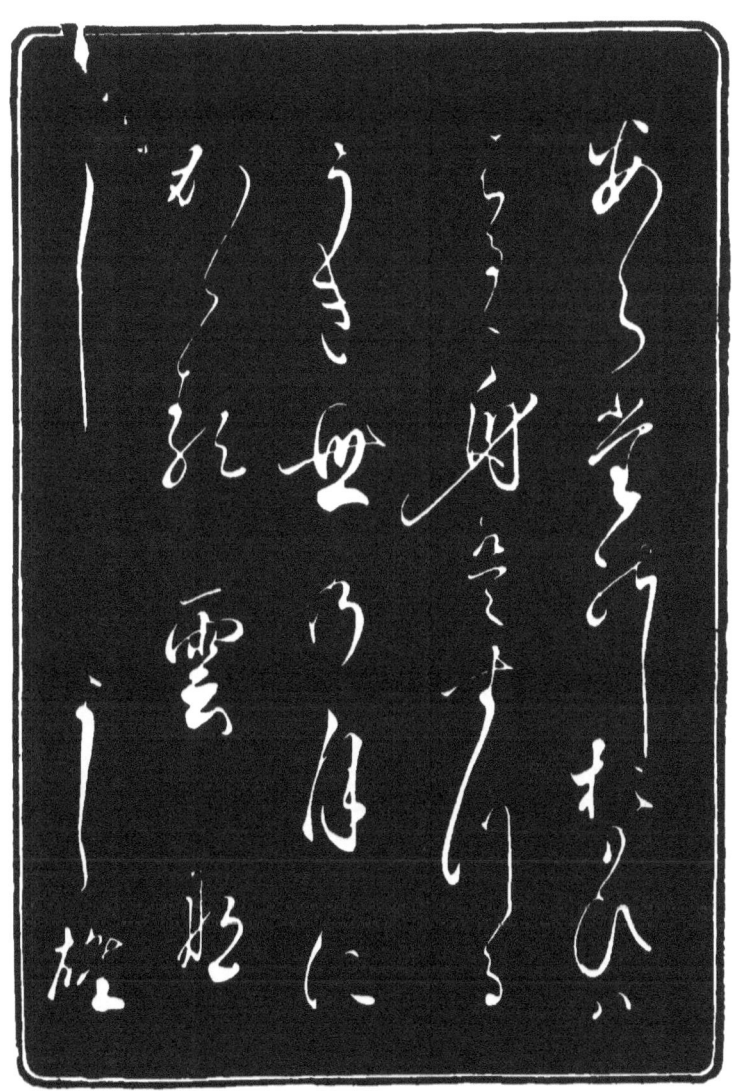

Last writing of Sir Big-rock.

" *Aru ureshi omoiwa haruru miwa sutsuru*
Ukiyens tsuki ni haharu kumonashi ".
Yoshio"

you for the many kindnesses we have enjoyed at your hands. Your benevolence has made us forget we were prisoners and emboldens us to ask this favor We desire that our bodies may find a resting-place near the tomb of our beloved chief. Could we be assured of this, we should die without a shadow of regret."

The *daimio*, who was greatly affected by this speech, thought for a moment and replied

" Unfortunately I have no authority in such a matter, yet I here pledge my honor to do everything in my power to bring about what you so ardently wish. Rest assured it shall be accomplished. I have now a favor to ask—a souvenir of yourself—which I will bequeath to my descendants as a precious relic."

Sir Big-rock went to the writing-stand, took up a brush and wrote :

" *Ara ureshi, omoiwa harura miwa sutzuru ;*
Ukiyono tzuki ni kakaru kumonashi."

(" I am indeed happy, for my desire is accomplished,
   though, in doing it, I have sacrificed my life.
The moon is no longer obscured by clouds.")

He then bowed respectfully and handed the paper to the *daimio*, who received it with many expressions of satisfaction.

As the noble ceased speaking, an officer entered and announced the arrival of the commissioners of the Sho-gun, whereupon Lord Narrow-river saluted the *ronin* and quitted the hall. After a brief interval, one of his councillors entered, and behind him came a number of retainers bearing white dresses and *kami-shimo* (ceremonial costumes), which they distributed among the prisoners, who were requested to prepare themselves for their sentence.

The *ronin* cast aside their garments and joyfully assumed the snowy robes; having done which they followed their guide to the audience chamber, where they found the commissioners and Lord Narrow-river, before whom they prostrated themselves and remained in the respectful attitude. The elder of the visitors took a paper from the bosom of his garment, and after glancing at Lord Narrow-river, read as follows :

" Big-rock, late Chief-councillor of Lord Morning-field, the *daimio* of Ako, and forty-six others.

" You, men, neither respecting the dignity of the city nor the laws of the country, having conspired against, broken by night into the house of, and slain, Sir Kira, the late master of ceremonies to the august Sho-gun, Iyetzuna, are, for your audacious conduct, hereby sentenced to perform *hara-kiri*. In addition to this your descendants are banished to the island of Oshima, there to remain during the pleasure of the authorities."

To this the *ronin* replied, as with one voice :

" We acknowledge the justice of our sentence and gratefully return our thanks for being permitted to die such an honorable death."

The commissioners quitted the hall and proceeded

to the residences of the *daimio* who had charge of the other *ronin*, to whom they likewise communicated the sentence.

At the hour of the Snake (10 A. M.) Sir Big-rock and his companions were kneeling in two rows upon thick mats placed in the court-yard of the *yashiki* of Lord Narrow-river, behind each *ronin* being two officers who were to act as their *kaishiyaku* (seconds).

In front of the condemned men knelt several *samurai* of the clan of Higo, who were present as witnesses for their lord.

At the same hour and moment a similar scene was enacted in the *yashiki* of Lord Pine-plain, Lord Mori, and Lord Water-field.

Sir Big-rock, whose face and bearing betokened the happiness that possessed his soul, turned to his companions and said in a loud, clear voice

"Comrades, we will now meet our last enemy!"

*   *   *   *   *   *   *

Before the sound of the temple bells had ceased to vibrate on the air, forty-six shadowy forms, headed by the spirit of Sir Big-rock, fell into line and began their march down the Lonely-Road.

Together they mounted the Hill of Death, together halted at the place where the three roads meet ; here they stripped off their white robes, which they handed to Sanzu-no Baba, and boldly plunging into the dark river, passed over to Gokuraku (Paradise), where they were welcomed by the spirit of their beloved chief.

CHAPTER XL.

THE RETURN OF THE EXILES.

"He, who is dutiful to his parents, will be loyal to his chief. A loyal man cannot fail to be patrotic."

The snows of eight winters had fallen upon the bamboos surrounding the cemetery of the Spring-hill Temple, where forty-seven tombs marked the resting-places of the loyal men of Ako.

On the morning of the 4th of February, 1710, a lady accompanied by two handsome young men, who carried in their hands bouquets of flowers, and followed by a servant, entered the enclosure and proceeded to a tomb which bore the inscription :

" *Zinkuan yoken shinshi.*"

(" A true samurai, who set an example to all and who used his sword where it was required.")

The visitors were the widow and sons of Sir Cliff-side, and the servant was Original-help, who had on that day returned from their place of exile and come to make offerings at the grave.

After sweeping the tomb, they burnt incense and repeated prayers, then proceeded to the temple where they found assembled many relatives and friends of the dead heroes, who, like themselves, had, by the accession of a new Sho-gun, been released from banishment.

When all had thanked the *Sojo* for the care he had bestowed upon the graves, they went to an adjoining apartment where they were shown the battered armor and weapons of the forty-seven *ronin*.

Among the party were the wife and two sons of Sir Big-rock, the wife and son of Sir Shell, the family of Sir Common, Miss Quiet, the betrothed of Sir Cliff-field, Lady Pine-island, and the loyal contractor, Noble-plain, whose participation in the conspiracy had caused him to be banished with the families of the *samurai*.

Mrs. Brilliant was not among the number, as on the day of her husband's death, she had joined him in paradise.

The visitors bowed before the souvenirs, which they regarded as good Buddhists do the relics ot their saints.

At the hour of the Snake (10 A.M.) the priests led the way to the chapel of the temple. When all had taken their places upon the matted floor, the venerable superior ascended the platform. and placing his hands upright, palm to palm, offered prayers, after which he thus addressed the congregation :

" How can I find words to express the feelings of

my heart. My aged tongue can but imperfectly speak the praises due to the loyal men, whose armor and weapons you have just worshiped ; who suffered so greatly and died so nobly. Oh, you are the favored ones; the gods have indeed been good to you; you are the descendants, relatives and friends of Immortals! Through all ages and changes, the names and fame of the loyal men, whose bodies rest beneath yonder tombs, will be remembered with respect and admiration. Their glorious deed will shine like a torch at night, and the whole world shall ring with their praise! They were dutiful sons, therefore were loyal men! They were loyal men, therefore were patriots! They have set an example which will be followed forever and ever, and the * day will surely come when their worth will be recognized in the highest place (by the Mikado). You, their sons, have an inheritance that will make you envied by all men. It is for you to follow in the footsteps of your fathers. You, widows, how glorious is your dower! You, friends of the departed heroes, how priceless your legacies! I salute you all, favored ones, and welcome you back from exile!"

He then briefly reviewed the lives of the forty-seven, pausing frequently to wipe the tears from his cheeks. His eloquence deeply moved the listeners, who, from time to time, uttered pious ejaculations and

---

* This prophecy has been fulfilled, H. I. M. Mutsuhito having in the year 1869 bestowed upon the tomb of Sir Big-rock the high honor of the Golden-leaf, thus recognizing the devotion of the loyal *ronin*.

bathed their sleeves with the dews of sorrow and joy.

When he had eulogized all the martyrs, he thus concluded his oration :

" The record of their sufferings, their heroism, and their loyalty, is engraved upon a golden tablet, and the friction of time, which obliterates most things, will only add lustre to their honorable names."

THE END.